Have a Dead Night

THE GROUNDSKEEPER TALES
BOOK FIVE

CEDAR SANDERSON

Copyright © 2025 by Cedar Sanderson

Cover Art & Design by Cedar Sanderson

Editing by Kathleen Sanderson and Liota Wakal

Copy-editing by Deb Hisle

All rights reserved.

No part of this book may be reproduced in any form or by any electronic or mechanical means, including information storage and retrieval systems, without written permission from the author, except for the use of brief quotations in a book review.

CONTENTS

1. Nightlife — 1
2. Morning Meeting — 11
3. Derp Kitty Dear — 23
4. Side Quest — 33
5. Root and Branch — 41
6. The Little Old Lady — 49
7. Curiosity and the Cat — 61
8. Sky and Trees — 71
9. Road Trip — 83
10. Weeping Bride Creek — 95
11. An Expedition — 105
12. Old Ghosts — 115
13. Cave of the Dead — 123
14. Missing Ghosts — 137
15. Bigfoot — 149
16. Unravelling — 163
17. Remembrance — 177
18. Postscript — 193

About the Author — 197
Also by Cedar Sanderson — 201
You might also like… — 205

To my baby bat, as always, and may you find your own path in life.

CHAPTER 1
NIGHTLIFE

The convenience store clerk barely looked up when the bell on the door tinkled. He knew who it was from the smell. Not the ripe, feculent aroma that went with a few of his customers. No, this one was dry like old leaves, with a musky dried-meat undertone. Out of his peripheral vision he saw the customer shambling towards the drinks cooler. Layers of clothing obscured what shape, if any, the person had.

After a moment, the customer approached the counter, head hanging so that the clerk couldn't see its face if he wanted to. A gnarled hand, pale as bone at the knuckles, pushed coins across the scarred glass.

The clerk didn't need to count them. He'd supplement them if it was short, and tuck some in a private stash if it were over.

"Thank you," he said. "Have a nice night."

"Have a dead night."

The customer was already shuffling towards the door, so the clerk wasn't entirely certain if he heard the response correctly.

The clerk shook his head as he finished ringing up the sale of the grape soda. "Have to have been *good* night," he muttered as he dropped the coins into their slots. At least this payment was clean, sometimes he got dirt and leaves with the coins from this customer. It was always coins.

The customer turned right after the heavy steel-and-glass door closed on the warmth and brightness of the store. The streetlamps worked here. Sometimes. One was flickering weakly. Shuffling, with much rustling from the dead leaves that worked as insulation between clothing layers, the shapeless pile of clothing headed up the hill, past the last working streetlamp, towards the cemetery.

Behind it, in the store, the clerk pulled his textbook and notepad back out onto the counter. Highlighter poised, he returned to his reading. One of the fluorescent lights near the cooler flickered a few times, before reluctantly returning to a weak, constant glow.

Chloe rolled over, off the couch and onto the floor with a thud. A book landed on top of her, adding insult to injury.

"Ouch." She sat up, rubbed her eyes, and looked at the time. "Oh no."

At least, she thought as she grabbed the stack of books, shoved them in her bag, and tossing a notebook and highlighter in after them, she didn't have to get dressed. She was already dressed from yesterday. Wearing nothing but black also meant it wasn't obvious they were the same clothes. Black ripped jeans, which hadn't been ripped when she bought them, black long-sleeved tee shirt with nothing cute printed on it...

Chloe pulled a brush through her hair, knowing if she looked in a mirror her roots would be showing a mile long by now. She hadn't had time for hair care, much less finding a more reliable purple dye... She twisted a band around her hair after coiling it into a messy bun, and ran out the door, scooping up the backpack as she went. She hadn't taken the time to make tea, or check the weather, so she found out it was raining as she clattered down the stairs from her apartment over the carriage house.

Winter was coming, and as usual it was starting off with a late fall filled with cold miserable rain. She held her backpack over her head as an improvised umbrella as she ran across the parking lot towards the big house. The library door opened as she arrived at it.

"Thanks." Chloe stepped in, onto a mat she didn't remember being there, and blinked as a skeleton handed her a towel. "Um?" She looked down. She was dripping wet. "Sorry, Della Dear. I didn't think about making puddles on your floor."

After blotting herself off and wiping her feet, Chloe finished her commute to the table at the center of the room. Della had disappeared soundlessly, as was her habit, and Mr. Cruor was not yet in evidence. Chloe pulled her books out of her backpack before tucking the bag itself into the footwell under her desk. She might be sitting there later, but the last few weeks had taught her it wasn't likely.

A single dead leaf on the rug caught her attention, and she scooped it up and into the trashcan, feeling guilty for having so nearly made a mess. It wasn't that Della minded, or not that much anyway, since she'd just met Chloe to make sure she was dried off; it was more that Chloe understood how hard Della worked. Della did for the inside what

Chloe had been doing for the outside until recently at Belleview.

Now, everything had changed. Chloe stood staring at the rain trickling down the outside of the windowglass. Last fall, this kind of day had been spent in the shed, cleaning tools, before retreating to her warm apartment with cocoa and a video game. Today was…

"Good morning," Mr. Cruor announced his arrival.

Chloe turned and smiled at him. He always looked so calm and collected. "Good morning, sir."

"I saw Della in the hall with the tea trolley," Mr. Cruor informed his apprentice. "Ah, there she is."

Della pushed the trolley through the open door and into the library where they would be working.

"Thank you, Della," Chloe told her. "I smell gingerbread!"

"Perfect on a day like this," Mr. Cruor waited until Della had poured. "And spiced chai. You must think we need warming up."

Della nodded her delicate ivory skull once before whisking away again, leaving Chloe and her boss to their morning ritual.

"I see you forgot your umbrella this morning." He sipped his tea.

"I was in a hurry." She had long since stopped wondering if he could see her as she crossed to the big house, or simply deduced from her general state of dampness. "And I didn't look first before leaving."

"Ah." He didn't really say anything, but Chloe sighed deeply.

"This is one of the lessons that doesn't come from books?" She laid a hand on the stack beside her. "Kind of like, being able to tell the difference between a lich and a wight means you left it too long and now it's too late to know what weapon you should have carried?"

"I rather think an umbrella would be useful in that instance." His voice was a murmur and he didn't meet her eyes as he meticulously ate a bite of the gingerbread, so dark, rich, and moist enough not to leave messy crumbles.

"It would?" Chloe was caught off guard by this answer. "How?"

"Element of surprise." He put down his fork and turned slightly, then mimed his actions as he spoke. "Pop open the umbrella, shield-like, then close rapidly, and repeat that cycle while retreating rapidly to a position where you can turn and run."

She blinked at him, her jaw dropped slightly. "That would work?"

"Neither creature possesses particularly good vision. By obscuring your true size and location it would, I believe, work. I did it by throwing up my arms, waving them wildly, while shouting."

He sipped his tea calmly. Chloe closed her open mouth with effort, made yet another mental note to never underestimate her boss, and picked up her own teacup. It really was a good socially acceptable way to break up an awkward space in a conversation.

"What *is* on the agenda for the day?" Chloe asked once the moment had passed.

"We have a meeting later this morning, and then, I believe you should take the afternoon off."

Chloe opened her mouth to object automatically, thought of a long-delayed shower, and closed it again. Mr. Cruor gave her his enigmatic smile.

"How is, ah, the Drama-Llama?"

He was referring to her pet hognose snake, a farewell

gift from a former teacher who'd encountered the supernatural and been broken by it.

"Estivating, I think." Chloe shrugged. "He's usually pretty sluggish after a feeding, for a week or so. So it may just be torpidity, but it's late enough in the year.."

"And Derp Kitty?"

Chloe felt the warmth rising in her cheeks. In her defense, she hadn't named the cheetah, or the snake, but the pet names coming from her formal boss's mouth emphasized the ridiculously silly words.

"I haven't been to see him for a few days. Rosa texted a video of him fetching a ball, though."

"How is The Abomination running?"

This name *was* her fault. Chloe shook her head. "Fine, I think?" The battered Land Rover had come along with her new position, but she hated driving. "I get the hint, sir. I'll go see Derp after lunch." She could shower after that, because she'd be covered in fur and the big cat's peculiar musk. She loved the Derp Kitty, but learned to be very glad the cheetah couldn't live in her tiny one-bedroom apartment with her.

"Very good." He finished his tea. Setting the cup down, he spoke more briskly, signaling a change to professional matters. "We will be meeting jointly with Detective Murray."

Chloe remembered him. The detective had thought she was not much older than his daughter. "Is this still about the wraith nest?"

"No, I don't believe they are even past the preliminary survey of that property."

"Right." Chloe wasn't sure she would even have noticed unusual activity outside Belleview, she'd been so busy. Or, for that matter, activity inside Belleview, which was more worrying to her.

"There will be some paperwork, and then we will go over a few active investigations with you."

Chloe blinked in surprise. "With me?"

"Yes, as you are now my successor." He lifted a finger. "I know you are uncomfortable with your role, Miss Brandt, but the fact remains. You have much to learn."

"So be quiet and keep my ears open?" Chloe knew she'd been arguing too much recently. She no longer felt like she'd been scooped up by a whirlwind. More like a hurricane.

"Your input will be valued."

Della returned for the breakfast things. Interrupted by this, Chloe moved her books to her desk, thinking the meeting would require their worktable to be cleared. She looked out the window, where it continued gray and rainy and would be until the snow came sometime later that month, unless she missed her guess.

Chloe looked at the time, then collected the book she'd been working through, and her notebook, before settling into one of the comfortable armchairs. Her desk had a view of the window; Mr. Cruor's desk stood at a right angle to hers, with bookshelves over it reaching to the ceiling. Their working table stood in the center of the room, with four chairs around it, and here, tucked into the corner formed by a projecting bookcase, were two worn upholstered chairs. She had never seen her boss sitting on them. Chloe opened the book to her bookmark and started a fresh page on the notebook. Her boss insisted on handwritten notes for two reasons. First, he'd told her, she would remember best what she handwrote rather than typed. Secondly, and more importantly, some of the books in the library were held securely. None of their content should be entered onto a machine with internet access.

Surrounded by books, warm, and dry, Chloe laughed silently at herself for missing the work outdoors in the cold and wet. She could get used to this as a job. Especially, with the option to play in the gardens when it was sunny.

CHAPTER 2
MORNING MEETING

Della had laid on the tea and departed just before Mr. Cruor ushered the detective into the library. Chloe was pretty sure the detective did not know about the housekeeper, Trunk, and likely the rest of the cemetery denizens. Chloe was standing to greet him, and he shook her hand.

"I remember you, it hasn't been that long. And now you're read in, eh?"

"Yes, sir." Chloe had decided that from context he meant the oath to the Brotherhood of Death. "I am."

"Miss Brandt is my successor in training, Detective Murray," Mr. Cruor took his seat; Murray sat to his left, and Chloe sat across from her boss. "I understand that will entail paperwork."

"Yes." Murray had a slim case from which he was removing a stack of paper. "Almost everything else in the world is online and electronic, but not when it comes to you, Cruor. Strictly burn-before-reading."

Chloe started to object that burning first would mean … and stopped herself from saying anything.

Murray gave her a quick wink. "Now, I'm assuming she'll need the same set-up you have. Expert consultant, vague bullshit, nobody says nothing about psychics."

"Indeed." Mr. Cruor poured out tea.

"I am not," Chloe spoke up this time. "A psychic."

"Of course not, that's why we don't say you are." Murray handed her papers. "Read these. Initial and sign. Happy to take questions."

Obediently, Chloe started to do as she was told. She was aware that while she was poring over forms which excused the police force of any and all liability in the course of her consultation with them, the two men were talking about Murray's family, and when they started in on sports, she tuned them out.

As she progressed through the papers, Chloe was surprised to learn she would be paid for her work if and when she was called on to consult. She looked up, caught Mr. Cruor's eye, and he nodded slightly. She signed, moving on. Getting paid twice sounded like a nice perk, if you could get it, and evidently she could. She stacked the papers neatly and looked at Detective Murray.

"All done? No problem with the NDA?"

Chloe shook her head. She couldn't talk about the Brotherhood outside of a select few, and anything she did with the police would fall under that umbrella.

"I can believe you'll keep it, too, you're so quiet." He took the papers from her and slipped them back into the case. "So, that's out of the way, let's talk business."

This time he gave folders to both of them. "Miss Brandt, I don't know how much your boss has filled you in on his work with us, yet."

"Not at all," Mr. Cruor answered for her. "We had been busy with theory and foundations. I have, in the past, made certain she understood that investigations move slowly, very methodically, and that our role sets us in a position outside the path, where we see very little of the investigators' machinations." Her boss caught Chloe's eyes. "And we have to be satisfied with that."

"Yes," Chloe spoke quietly into the space following her boss's firm statement.

"Well, you're doing better than I would be. But then again, not being able to drop it is why I'm a detective, I guess."

"I don't have a choice," Chloe shrugged. "And I've learned that sometimes it wouldn't be safe to keep chasing my curiosity."

"And yet, you do it anyway." Cruor murmured, sipping tea.

Detective Murray looked at her for a long moment. Chloe could feel herself blushing.

"How much do you know about the mass grave under a certain house?" he asked, finally.

"Some." She shrugged. "Have you ever seen a ghost, sir?"

"I'll deny I ever said this, and I wouldn't say it outside of this room, but I've seen some things which are really difficult to explain. I think anyone in my line of work has. We don't talk about it. We pretend we didn't. But I landed with this liaison, and things got really hard to ignore."

Chloe nodded her understanding. "I hadn't before I came to Belleview. Now, I talk to them regularly, and mostly they're just people."

Detective Murray shuddered. "Sorry. The way you said that gave me the creeps."

"She isn't wrong, however. They were human. Some of the other things..." Mr. Cruor set his cup down. "I respect that you would rather not know, Detective. However, that does not make them any less real."

"Yeah, well, this one," Murray jerked his head in Chloe's direction. "She's so young, and, well, it seems wrong."

"I don't argue her youth. However, sometimes those who can break a paradigm are those new to the field. They have not internalized what is normal. They will question the accepted answers."

"Nothing," the detective muttered, "is normal about this."

"Isn't that why they call it paranormal?" Chloe asked, curious. "We," she gestured to Belleview around them, the house, its occupants, "are outside of the norms?"

The detective sighed, noisily. "That you are. And for all that it's weird and I try not to think about it, you get results."

"So, what have you brought us now?" Mr. Cruor changed the subject, looking at the folder he'd been given. Chloe had three.

"A new puzzle. And for you, Miss Brandt, the puzzle pieces you've already been involved with."

"Thank you." Chloe realized she had been handed the files on her crying ghost's victims, and the jawbone of the hoodoo skull. That latter file was very slim, being a bare three pages, mostly details on where the bone had turned up and a page of a medical examiner's report.

"Don't expect answers anytime soon on the bone. It's illegal to traffic in human remains, but without evidence of foul play, further testing isn't happening. Budget constraints."

This was what Mr. Cruor had told her already, so Chloe just nodded and opened the thicker file, the one with the new case.

"I, personally, don't think there's anything to this. As you'll see in the file, it's a nervous old lady. We've responded, and by we, I mean patrol, until the last call, about fifty times over the last two years to her house. She's convinced she has a stalker."

"And you don't think so."

"Nothing shows on the camera." Murray shrugged. "But just in case, because her nephew is my boss, we've called in the ghostbusters."

"Which is us?" Chloe looked up from her reading.

"You're probably too young for that reference."

"I'm not." She smiled. "My parents gave me an education."

He laughed. "Good for them. So, yeah, I fully expect this one to be a cakewalk."

"Good training." Mr. Cruor didn't look up as he spoke.

"Point there, I suppose. I don't know what changed, but this last call I went out there with my partner," he looked at Chloe, "who is not read in. We had a long talk with Mrs. Buchanan, and I have to say, she creeped me out. So there may be something in it, but these cases are not out of the normal, if you know what I mean."

"I do, and you are correct that most of the time nerves fool the mind into seeing more than is there. It is not, however, something which should be dismissed and ignored."

Murray's face went serious. "No." He looked at Chloe. "You into true crime?"

Chloe shook her head. She'd always found the true crime stuff to be overly dramatic for her taste, and also, just plain nosy.

"Right. So there's a famous case of a woman who was stalked. For years, she went through life looking over her shoulder; she was abducted and then released. She was blamed for doing it just to get attention. And then," Murray shook his head. "She was killed. By her stalker. The cops had blown her off, over and over, and had even said she was doing it all herself. Rules got changed. We take stuff like this," he tapped the folder. "More seriously now."

"So, what can we do to help?" Chloe asked.

"Not much." Detective Murray flipped his hand like he was tossing something away from him. "You can't appear in court, so your word isn't evidence. You can't collect clues, but as I understand, you can follow them."

"We can rule out the abnormal," Mr. Cruor added. "Which is sometimes very useful. And occasionally, we can confirm that there is a paranormal element, which is generally not helpful other than allowing the case to be shelved."

"Yeah, it's not that we want to have another cold case, sometimes that's just where the trail runs out and we stop. Does help to know, personally, there's no way to bring that one to justice in the courts and all."

Chloe considered this. "So, don't touch anything, keep my eyes and ears open, and if there is a tangible clue, bring you to it."

"You've got it."

Chloe looked at Mr. Cruor. She wasn't sure how much she could talk about in front of the detective. Mr. Cruor shook his head a tiny bit, and she left it for a later, private chat.

"When would you like us to pay Mrs. Buchanan a visit? And what pretext will we be under?"

"Soon; it's been a couple of weeks since the last call, so we're due." Murray eyed Chloe. "I have no idea how to explain you."

"So don't," Mr. Cruor suggested. "I can explain her, if asked, as a student."

"She's no stranger than most college students, I guess." Detective Murray tidied up his case. "I'll introduce you as the researcher, then."

"It is true, and truth covers a great deal of ground."

"I'll make the calls." Murray stood up. "Miss Brandt, a pleasure. Also, so you know, the old lady usually calls at two in the morning."

"The witching hour." Mr. Cruor stood to escort the man out. "When most of the living world lies profoundly sleeping."

When Mr. Cruor returned, alone, Della was clearing the tea things.

"You had many thoughts, Miss Brandt. I could see them chasing one another across your face."

Chloe sighed. "I'm that transparent?"

"At times, yes."

"What if..." She paused for a breath. "What if something else committed a crime? Not human?"

"Then it falls into our jurisdiction, Miss Brandt, not into the police's business. Detective Murray is a good man, and not a linear thinker, as any good detective should never be. However, he is determined that the paranormal should not exist and so, for him, it does not."

"Then why does he work with you?" Chloe tilted her head slightly to one side. "And now, me?"

"I've been able to give him leads which developed into answers he could accept. For that, he'll put up with a lot. I rather think he views me as a sort of Sherlock Holmes, detecting the inscrutable in a manner which may look like magic but is in reality a science."

Chloe pondered this, slouching into her chair. "It doesn't obey the laws of physics," she finally muttered.

Mr. Cruor nodded. "It may, but at a quantum level most do not understand, and he certainly would not. However, that is outside the scope of our work, Miss Brandt. I will draw your attention to the word I used initially. Jurisdiction. A definition, please."

"The word of the law?" She sat up. "Wait, the Brotherhood has a court?"

"Not quite the word, but the speaking of law. It is also a term used to define a territory, and within those limits, the authority over it. The Brotherhood of the Dead has the authority over the dead."

"What about Horace?" Chloe was thinking rapidly of the denizens of the cemetery, those she considered under her care, first at the Groundskeeper, and now, as whatever she was. Mediator.

"Horace is a... he is not dead, so he would not fall under our authority, except that, like Trunk, he has sought sanctuary in Belleview, which does bring him under that umbrella."

"Huh." Chloe was staring at the table. "And Padraig, Hugh... any other fairytale creatures I don't know about yet?"

"A great many of those are, indeed, only figments of active imaginations. Or misunderstandings of one kind, spun into many tales."

"But there are more. And whatever is bothering Mrs. Buchanan could be something like that. What do we do then?"

"You're asking if there is another layer of sub-rosa enforcement, like the Brotherhood?" Mr. Cruor was now the one doing the head tilt. Chloe wondered if she'd picked it up from him.

"Yes?"

"There is not." Mr. Cruor wasn't focused on her; he was looking over her head as though he were seeing something not there. "There was, yes."

"Oh. And so, that's us, isn't it?"

"Indeed, Miss Brandt. It may not have been in the job description originally, however…" His lips crooked up just a little.

"I know how that goes. First, you're mowing lawns, and then suddenly you find yourself on a stakeout looking for figments."

He chuckled. "Since the future is uncertain, I strongly suggest that you go get lunch, make your visit to a certain large kitty, and then sleep early."

"I'll do that." Chloe got her backpack and started tucking books into it, then changed her mind and left some of them on her desk. "I'll dial back the homework tonight."

"Excellent. I will see you in the morning, not before."

"Unless there's a phone call." She put her hand on the doorknob. "How does that work?"

"I will call you. We will meet at the car fifteen minutes after that. How are you at waking and dressing in a hurry?"

Chloe remembered how she'd woken up that morning. "I'll be ok."

"Right, then. Perhaps tonight will not be the night."

CHAPTER 3
DERP KITTY DEAR

Her hair still wet, but twisted up and skewered in place with a pair of chopsticks, having finally managed her shower, Chloe left the cemetery that afternoon on her errand. She carefully maneuvered the Abomination through traffic as she approached the zoo. She wouldn't be parking where visitors were, which was easy enough to get to. Instead she got to go in the back way where the narrow streets made it tighter than she liked to get to the back gate. Chloe was anxious and cranky by the time she parked. As she walked up to the back guardhouse she wondered if they would even let her in … To her great relief, she was expected, and once inside, quickly made her way to meet Rosa, Derp Kitty's keeper.

"Hey, girl!" Rosa hugged her. She was shorter than Chloe, rounder, but Chloe knew from hugging her and watching Rosa work with her cats that the older woman was heavily muscled under her curves. "You can't stay away this long. He gets down and missin' you!"

"He only knew me for a few days," Chloe protested, but

didn't slow down as they headed for the enclosure where the Derp Kitty was waiting. She missed him, too.

"Well, you made an impression." Rosa unlocked the door and they stepped into the fenced area.

Rosa whistled, and Chloe called, "Derp! Come here, Derp!"

Rosa laughed as the caramel-and-black blur appeared out of nowhere to jump up and give Chloe an enthusiastic purring greeting. "That's a terrible name."

"Yeah," Chloe managed, once Derp collapsed none-too-gracefully to reveal his belly for scratching. "But it's so accurate."

"He's such a love." Rosa joined in on the session, while Derp purred like a sack full of running chainsaws. "I don't think I've ever handled a cat like him. He's like... like a Golden Retriever got in a cheetah costume and the zipper stuck."

Chloe laughed. "He even plays fetch!"

"Yes he does, until I get tired and have to stop." Rosa stood, went to a basket mounted onto the wall, and came back with a giant tennis ball. Or, as Chloe discovered, a ball made to look like a tennis ball complete with the yellow fuzz, somewhat shredded loose by a certain cat's large teeth. "So you get to be the dummy today!"

Chloe held the ball up and Derp jumped to his feet. With both hands, she hurled it as far as she could, and watched the speedster do his thing. Running, he was far more graceful than he was in any other motion. He grabbed the ball and returned to her, his tail high.

"He really does look like a dog when he does that."

"Some of the other big cats will play fetch, but they usually outgrow it and get bored with it fast even when they do," Rosa told her. "This one, though, I haven't yet seen him tire of it. He's probably bored, as well as lonely, poor baby. But he can't have company, he's too accustomed to humans."

Chloe wasn't sure how much Rosa knew about where Derp Kitty had come from. For that matter, Chloe wasn't sure how much socialization Derp had there, with the dead lions and the leopard John had been afraid was loose. Chloe certainly wasn't going back to ask Rada Orban any questions. She would talk to Igone; grumpy old men didn't frighten her, but she would just get angry with Rada, who'd killed her pets for no real reason. Anger at a ghost, Chloe had decided, did no good.

"That's too bad," was all she said to Rosa. "I will do my best to get here more often." She wrinkled her nose. "I hate driving in city traffic."

"You hate driving. I've seen you in that thing, and I don't blame you!"

"The Abomination isn't the problem." Chloe shook her head. "It's all the other drivers!"

Rosa laughed, and they played with Derp until Chloe begged exhaustion, and a need for an early night. The cheetah showed no signs of being tired at all, but was willing to repeat belly rubs as she said goodbye to him.

Chloe drove home again, covered in cheetah fur, and regretting that she lived in a food desert. It would be almost an hour out of her way, with traffic, to go to the big grocery store and stock up. She needed to stock up. Tonight was not the night. She was heading up the hill for the main gates when she decided she'd at least get snacks. She pulled into the gas station and convenience store, under the working side of the fuel pump canopy, and topped off the tank. Not knowing when or where she'd be going was reinforcing her mother's stringent requirements to fill up at anything under a half-tank of gas. Chloe screwed the cap back on until it clicked, grinning to herself as she remembered one vacation spent partly on the side of the road when they'd run dry because her father had been playing chicken with the Empty light. Chloe and her siblings had been just fine with it, because there was a creek alongside the road, and in the creek were minnows and crawdads to chase and catch. Her mother had been furious, then laughed as she'd thrown up her hands and stated she'd won that argument, categorically.

Chloe headed into the convenience store. She was telling herself she'd earned junk food. Inside, the clerk didn't look up at her. He was running a highlighter over the page of an open textbook. It reminded Chloe she wanted to spend an hour studying that night, even if she was mostly taking the night off.

Chloe grabbed a couple bags of chips, a soda, and a candy bar before heading to the counter. The clerk, a shaggy-haired young man not much older than she was, if that, shoved his book out of sight.

"Whatcha studying?" Chloe asked while he rang her things up.

He lifted his head, eyes wide behind the fringe of curly brown hair, like he was seeing her for the first time. "Business admin."

"Nice. Practical." She pushed her debit card into the reader. "Good luck!"

"Yeah. Thanks." He put her purchase into a plastic bag. "Receipt?"

"Not tonight. Have a good one."

She was almost out the door when he responded. "Have a dead night."

Chloe climbed into Abomination, puzzling over that

one. Maybe he knew she worked at the cemetery and was trying to be funny. She was getting better about putting herself out into social situations, though; she was happy about that. She'd even managed to compliment him, and got what was almost a smile. She could see why her parents made a point of doing things like that.

Back at her apartment, she put the things she'd bought away, other than the drink and one bag of chips, then set a timer for fifteen minutes of housecleaning. When she'd first moved in here, living on her own had felt fun. She'd stopped cleaning up after herself because she had the freedom to let it fall wherever. After an incident where someone almost saw the mess, she'd realized it made her feel like crap, she had decided she wasn't going to let it get that bad again. If she took a few minutes every day, it wouldn't take hours to reclaim her life.

Without dirty dishes in the sink mocking her, rewarding herself with soda, chips, and an hour of gaming felt good. Going to bed at a reasonable hour and clean was also good. Waking up after midnight with a jolt, though ...

Chloe lay there in the dark staring at the ceiling. She wasn't sure if she'd heard something, or if it had only been in her dream, which she couldn't quite remember now that she was awake. It only took her a minute of listening to the silence before she got out of bed. Checking the time, it was half-past midnight. No new notifications showed on her phone when she picked it up off her desk. The open concept of her apartment made it easy to see she was alone. The door was still locked. She stood in the middle of the room for a moment, then returned to bed. It had to have been a dream.

Falling back to sleep wasn't as easy, though. She'd resisted the urge to bring the phone into her warm blanket nest. Sleep hygiene mattered, her mother had emphasized. Screens in bed were the worst. Chloe sighed into the darkness. She knew what she was supposed to do, but sometimes she wanted to just do the things she knew not to do.

Morning came as a surprise, when her alarm chirped from across the room, and she rolled out of bed before her brain fully engaged. The heat lamp glowed over the Drama Llama, set on to keep her snake buddy safe and happy. This gave her enough light to make her way across the apartment. Chloe hit the button to start her kettle as she staggered towards the phone to silence its interruption of her deep sleep state.

With the device out of sleep mode, she still saw no notifications that would indicate anything had happened in the night. Chloe made her tea and then prepared for her day. She checked the weather, both on the computer and by looking out a window, and saw that an umbrella wasn't called for. Yet. She put one with her bag just in case.

It was only when she was walking across the parking pad that she saw what must have awakened her in the night. One of the big trees at the edge of the lawn, marking the tenuous boundary where the house demesnes ended and the graves began, had dropped a big limb. Almost a third of its canopy was lying on the ground.

Chloe walked towards it, as she neared it the brown leaves of the fallen oak branch shivered, then parted.

"Dagnabbit." Padraig had his hands on his hips as soon as he popped out from under the branches, then turned to look up at the tree. "That's going to be a mess."

"Already a mess." Chloe joined him in looking upwards. "Is that …?"

"Hardware." He pointed with a stubby forefinger. "Someone put bolts in, tryin' to keep the branch up."

"I wonder how long ago that was." Chloe squinted. "Looks all rusty."

"That it does. Guess it worked for a while."

"This is going to take a chainsaw." Chloe contemplated the branch, almost as big around as her waist at the base. It had landed horizontally but that hadn't stopped the weight of it making a big scrape in the lawn turf. "And resodding."

Padraig rubbed his hands together. "More power!"

"Of course, they did cuts like this before chainsaws ..." Chloe contemplated the top of the garden gnome's head, covered with a thick woolen cap knitted from a faded red yarn.

"Going to kick if we aren't careful with cut placement." He shoved his cap back and scratched his balding head while he thought. "Hugh is a bit green. May need more hands for this."

"I can try to hire labor?" Chloe was fairly sure that would be a doomed attempt, she'd tried hiring for Belleview before and never even got applicants.

"Nah, call Eloise and summon the clan. Probably need transport, though." Padraig looked up at her, his bushy eyebrows lifted.

"I can drive The Abomination down that far by myself," Chloe responded with her best attempt at dignity. The gnome had ridden with her once, not long after she'd been re-taught how to drive. He'd ended that drive by falling to his knees and kissing the ground after he'd made his exit as soon as she put the Land Rover in park.

The gnome crossed himself. "Pretty sure that warrants danger pay."

"It does not. I've had more practice." Chloe pulled out her phone. "I need to check in with Mr. Cruor and see when I can go, then I'll call Eloise. What is on the task board?"

She and Padraig kept a running list on the white-board in the shed.

"Since it's not raining." He looked up at the sky and shook his fist in that direction. "Yet. I thought I'd try for the brush off the Nile."

She knew what he meant. The system of tiny roads internal to the cemetery had their own naming system. For that area it was all river names.

"Watch out for frogs." She headed for the library, leaving Padraig cackling behind her.

CHAPTER 4
SIDE QUEST

"Yes, I agree that chainsaws are unwise..." Mr. Cruor was standing on the landing outside the library door, looking at the fallen tree branch from a distance. "And certainly, asking for more manpower is a good idea, if Eloise can spare them for a day or two."

"I told Padraig I'd be able to drive over and get them." Chloe knew the gnomes had their own secret ways of getting around. She also knew it would take them days to get across the city that way, because that's how Hugh and Ewan had made their way when they were first interviewing for the positions of her assistants. Padraig had beat them to the punch, but he was older and bolder.

"That would be helpful." Her boss looked down at her. "You are more confident driving, then."

"I don't like it, but it's much more convenient than taking the bus. And I can go places where there are no buses."

Like going to Eloise's place, which was as far west as you could go in the state. It was quite rural over that direction, once you got past the edge of the city sprawl. Chloe liked it once she was past the traffic.

"Talk to Eloise, and if she can spare them, you might see if you can go over there today." Mr. Cruor opened the door, and held it for Chloe to go back into the library. "I'd like to cover crime scene etiquette with you, since it seems like we will be making a police sanctioned visit soon."

"But we won't know it's a crime scene?"

"Ah, rule one. Always treat it like there has been a crime, and evidence will need to be collected. What do you know about the fruit of the poisoned tree, Miss Brandt?"

"So many rules, and now we're back to gardening again?" Chloe sat obediently at the table, pulling her notebook and pen closer to make this rule a header on a new page. She'd found sticky tabs, and they were proliferating as she tried to keep categories straight in the book.

Mr. Cruor chuckled. "This is a legal term. It refers to evidence which is improperly acquired, and which can taint later evidence. So it is very important to be cautious at any scene, whether we know a crime has been committed, or not."

"Don't touch, got it. That would be rule two." Chloe jotted it down. "Basically, look, try not to step on anything, and watch for ghosts."

"Yes, very succinct. Ghosts, or other things."

They had been going through books, sorting myths from their real basis so far as Mr. Cruor knew. He'd been firm that although he did have the collective records of the Brotherhood, there was no way to be sure some things didn't actually exist. Or, perhaps, did. No one had ever seen a unicorn, and he was fairly sure that was indeed a mistaken sighting of something like a gazelle from the side. Dragons, however, had existed. Chloe was sad to learn they were believed extinct now, and had been for three centuries.

"So, keep my head on a swivel. Rule three."

"You do come up with some interesting sayings." Mr. Cruor had sat down with his own notebook, although he wasn't writing.

"Oh, that's something my Mom's friend Jay says." Chloe looked up at him. "Are there more rules?"

"From here they are more like suggestions." Mr. Cruor riffled through the pages of the notebook he was holding. "Ah, here."

They spent about an hour going over the details of how to handle being very unusual consultants. He coached Chloe in how to answer questions without lying, but also without revealing anything that might unsettle those who did not need to know what the Brotherhood did, or what lay beyond their understanding of the world.

Eloise returned Chloe's call, and was willing to help.

"Padraig mentioned chainsaws …" Chloe told her.

Mr. Cruor could hear Eloise's response as Chloe pulled the phone away from her ear, wincing slightly.

"Oh my dear! Heavens, no. I'll send the crosscut saw with the clan. You'll have no end of volunteers if it means not giving Padraig a chainsaw."

A few moments later, Chloe ended the call and looked across the table at her boss. "I'm to come directly after lunch, she says."

"I heard." Mr. Cruor had gotten up and rung the bell for Della during the call. "I will let Trunk know his afternoon class has been postponed."

Chloe was still studying the history and geology of the region with the bridge troll in the basement. "Tell him I'm sorry to miss it. We were going to cover the lidar of the ghost river today."

"Really? How fascinating."

"It's public data," Chloe explained. "We were both happy to see that the lidar map of the cemetery doesn't show anything we didn't already know about."

"How detailed is it?"

"Not very, but I think that may be a good thing."

"You are correct."

They both looked up as Della opened the door and rolled the trolley into the library. Chloe hastily cleared her books off the table, while Mr. Cruor retreated with great dignity to his own desk until the housekeeper had set the table for them.

After lunch, Chloe climbed into the Abomination and set up her gear, drinks, and snacks for driving. There was a phone mount to show her a heads-up display of a map, and a radio transmitter to play tunes, since the vehicle was far too old for bluetooth connection. As a matter of fact, the stereo system was so basic it hadn't even played anything: radio only. Someone, likely Rada Orban, had installed an aftermarket kit which supplied power to a device, otherwise Chloe wouldn't have been able to even use her phone for the GPS. Once she was comfortable, she set off on her trip.

By traveling in the middle of the day she was able to avoid most of the traffic, and once she got on the ring road, Chloe was out of the city rapidly. She didn't really relax and enjoy the drive until she'd left that highway and gotten onto the back road which took her, arrow-straight, through cornfields. Clouds in the blue sky were children's-book perfect, their bottoms as flat as though they sat on a glass plate high overhead.

Eloise's home, a small cottage in the middle of a large garden, was easy to see, coming as it did in a break in the fields. The trees which sheltered it from the road loomed up above the soybeans like a beacon. Chloe slowed, signaled, and turned, even though the road was barely more than one lane here and she'd never seen another car on this part of the road.

Eloise was in the garden, wearing a loose calico dress with an apron over it, and she straightened slowly, waving to her visitor. Chloe didn't see gnomes, but she knew they were there. She had come to realize that Padraig was odd if for no other reason than he allowed himself to be seen, instead of mysteriously appearing when needed.

"Hello!" Chloe called as she climbed down from her trusty rusty steed.

"You are doing so well!" Eloise came to her, hands out.

Chloe gently squeezed the old lady's hands and followed the motion with a hug as Eloise pulled her closer. Eloise had helped her re-learn to drive after John had given up in a lesson. Eloise's quiet reassurance had allowed Chloe to build confidence, not freeze in terror.

"I'm trying to practice. I don't like it, but..."

"It's independence, on four wheels," Eloise nodded as she let go and studied Chloe at arm's length. "You have regained your equilibrium?"

"I guess?" Chloe shrugged. "I realized this job has perks."

"Such as?" Eloise linked one of her arms with Chloe, and they slowly walked towards the house.

"Not having to work in the cold rain?" The weather, having cleared, was sunnily trying to remove some of the chill from the air. "And I get paid to research?"

"There will be times in the rain," Eloise chuckled. "But

not as many as the groundskeeper role, I concede. Tell me about this fallen tree while I get cocoa ready."

Chloe understood this to mean briefing the unseen gnomes, since she had told Eloise over the phone. She sat at the kitchen table, spoke louder than she really needed to, and watched Eloise put on the kettle, not the doors where she might have seen motion.

"It's the really big old oak to the south of the house, and one of the limbs came down in last night's storm. At the base, it's as big around as I am. Looks like there was an arborist repair at some point, well before my time, because there are two rusty bolts which would have been installed between it and the trunk."

Eloise tsked at this, shaking her head. Chloe went on as mugs were filled with homemade cocoa powder.

"Padraig suggested chainsaws. I don't think I have one big enough to deal with that big a branch, and anyway..." There was a small sound behind her, hard to guess if it was a gasp or a laugh quickly extinguished, "I suggested they must have had tools from the time before chainsaws which could do it, and we'd have them in the shed."

The shed, big enough to be a pole barn on another property, had been a mess when Chloe arrived. She could see, once she cleared paths, the remains of organization, but until Padraig, Ewan, and Hugh had taken it up, she hadn't made a great deal of progress out there. It was clear that previous groundskeepers had never thrown anything away which might still be useful.

"We seem to have more than one cross-cut saw," Chloe told Eloise now. "But this is going to be a big job for the four of us, and I'm on call for ... a thing that may come in the middle of the night."

"Oh really, so you are going straight into that line of work." Eloise put the steaming mug in front of Chloe.

Chloe sniffed deeply. Cinnamon, and a hint of orange. Eloise blended her cocoa with all sorts of wonderful flavors, and it was always rich, not too sweet, and creamy.

"I guess?" Chloe took a sip and closed her eyes. "Mmmm…"

"It's not always part of service to the Brotherhood." Eloise was beaming when Chloe opened her eyes again. She liked people to enjoy her little experiments.

"It isn't?"

"No," Eloise shook her head, firmly. "I haven't ever worked with the police… directly."

"So, it's just Mr. Cruor and John?"

"John is bi-vocational, dear, and his job is with the police, in a manner of speaking; as a member of the Brotherhood he is just very well placed."

"Well, I'm officially a police consultant now." Chloe knew she sounded glum. She felt uncertain of her usefulness in that role.

"And expecting a call in that capacity," Eloise nodded. "Which limits your availability for the clean-up job."

"I'd rather not give Padraig a chainsaw."

"He can be a bit… enthusiastic." Eloise's eyes were focused somewhere under Chloe's elbow, now. "Otherwise, how has he been?"

"Very helpful."

A deep, gravelly voice came from right beside her. "He bloody well oughta be."

Chloe jumped. Even knowing the gnomes had been listening, she hadn't expected one to pop up *right there.*

Unruffled, Eloise proceeded to introductions.

"Lochlainn, this is Chloe. Chloe, this is the head of the clan."

"Pleased to meet you," Chloe put out her hand, and the short gnome with a silver beard shook it gravely.

He was older than Padraig, she thought, but it was hard to tell. White hair, or what she could see of it under his red peaked cap, a beard that obscured most of his face aside from the tip of his nose and the dark beady eyes shadowed by bushy brows and the rolled edge of his cap.

"So you're the younker at Belleview." He had been surveying her while she assessed him. Chloe wondered what he made of a young woman in all black, from her jeans to her tee shirt to her boots, with black eyeshadow and to top it off, pastel lavender hair with chestnut roots showing badly. She needed to redo her purple before it faded entirely. "T'boys say you did a job of work there on your own."

"Which is a compliment, dear," Eloise put in before Chloe could decide what he'd meant.

"Aye. Now, tell me more aboot t'branch."

CHAPTER 5
ROOT AND BRANCH

Driving home with Lochlainn and three other gnomes she'd never even seen was a much quieter experience. At least it was contra-rush hour, so she was coming into the city as most were fleeing it for their homes and refuges for the evening. Chloe had opened the rear doors, then climbed into her own seat, Lochlainn taking shotgun beside her, then waited, eyes front, until the rear doors closed.

She'd announced to no one in particular that seatbelts were required, then after hearing *sotto voce* grumbles, but more importantly, metallic clicking, she'd started the vehicle and not for the first time, blessed Eloise's foresight in having her driveway end in a loop. Chloe really hated backing the Abomination up, and she wasn't at all sure how the gnomes would deal with her craning her neck to see out the back window while she did so.

Chloe didn't play her music, since she wasn't sure how her passengers would feel about symphonic metal or EDM, and there wasn't a good way to poll them since most of them couldn't even bring themselves to be seen, much less heard. Chloe was sympathetic. She'd felt that way most of her life.

It was only very recently that she'd started to make an effort to get out of that safe little box she'd packed herself into. If it hadn't been for the job, the new one, the one that involved being part of a top-secret organization which didn't officially exist ... Chloe sighed, then laughed softly. Lochlainn, sitting next to her, hunkered down where he wouldn't show over the dashboard, gave her side-eye but didn't say anything.

As she pulled off the ring road and started on the last leg towards Belleview, Chloe wondered what they would do if she were pulled over. She was being cautious about speed; she always was. According to John, too cautious. But what if there was a light out on the Abomination? Or something? How would the gnomes react to a policeman walking up and looking at them? Chloe decided not to ask Lochlainn and alarm the gnomes. She'd ask Padraig. He put up with her being curious, and seemed happy to chat. From him, she knew the clan was very cautious about being seen by humans, which is why she rarely saw Ewan or Hugh, and never heard them speak. She'd also learned a lot about Belleview, as it had been long before she came to live there.

Chloe signaled, and carefully turned into the big gate. Lochlainn straightened up a bit, enough to look around. She couldn't read an expression on his face in her peripheral vision, but he seemed curious.

"The garden shed's behind the stables." She pointed at the long building which she lived above. "There's a toilet in there, and likely Padraig'll meet you."

Behind her, the doors opened, and after a moment of shuffling, closed again. Lochlainn looked up at her. "Thank'ee for the ride."

"Thank you, all of you, for the help." She smiled and nodded at him. "I take it I should leave the crew to it?"

"Would be easiest, miss."

She sighed. "I understand, but I do miss getting my hands dirty."

He snorted. "You're no proper one, then. You're a right sort."

Then he too was gone, closing the door politely behind him, leaving her wondering just what he'd just said to her.

Either the brief time of blue skies and sun visible had ended, or it simply never cleared here at Belleview; Chloe wasn't sure. The light was dim already, even though there were a couple of hours until official end of daylight. The air nipped at her cheeks, and she looked around at the leafless trees (the fallen oak had still been covered in leaves but they were the dark brown of late autumn). It could snow. She didn't think it would, but it wasn't too early in the year.

She put the Abomination away in the garage bay designated for it. In the bay next to it, the black sedan Mr. Cruor drove gleamed in the dark. Past it, hidden in shadows, was a hearse which she longed to drive, from the 1930s and all curves and black satin. Beyond it was a Victorian relic, a horse-drawn hearse which was maintained, although horses would have to be hired to take it out. Trunk lamented that they wouldn't be able to find a matched four blacks with no white on them. To her surprise, when Chloe asked about it, she'd learned that once in a great while it was taken out, for a parade usually, and that Mr. Cruor drove it when this happened, but it hadn't for four or five years now.

The stables had been renovated for the cars, horse stalls removed, the corrals behind the stables turned into lawn, and from the maps Trunk had showed her, part of the area dedicated to keeping horses had been turned into gravesites. Above the stables the grooms' apartments had been kept, which allowed her living quarters, as well as a shared apartment currently occupied by the gnomes. Chloe had never heard them, even with a shared wall. Their entrance was on the other end of the building.

She checked her messages, and found one from Mr. Cruor recommending she get an early night, and another from Trunk with an assignment for their class the next day. Chloe went up to her apartment, took care of biological needs, then hunted for the books she'd need to write the essay. She had one, but the other was on her desk in the library.

By then, it was twilight, and the rain was starting off with a light drizzle. She took her umbrella. Opening the umbrella as she left the covered stairs, Chloe was thinking of the conversation she'd had with Mr. Cruor about using it as a distraction device. She walked across the rain-wet asphalt, and when a shadow moved at the edge of the lawn, she startled.

"Hey?" A voice came from the shadows. "Din't mean to scare you..."

"Benny." Chloe knew all her exasperation came through. "Why are you here?"

"Just... checking in. You haven't been by in a while."

"I have been busy." She walked closer, but not too close to the ghoul. His body odor was breathtaking. "I'm sorry. You ok?"

It was still part of her job, and likely would be for the rest of her life, taking care of the residents of Belleview. Living, dead, and maybe?

"Yeah. Just checking." He shuffled. "Horace says he's out o' food for Goldie."

"I'll bring him some, but she's not going to be eating much with the water so cold." Chloe propped the umbrella between her cheek and shoulder while she made a note. The water nymph and his fat fish, Goldie Spawn, lived in the biggest fountain at the top of the hill. "Anything else I need to know? I appreciate you keeping an eye out, since I've been in training so much."

"Training?" Benny was standing on one leg, then the other, in his usual jittery poses.

"Yeah, but don't worry, I'm still working at Belleview."

There was a momentary silence. Chloe resisted the urge to elaborate on her explanation. Benny didn't need to know, and he was the cemetery gossip. Which made him useful to her, but she didn't care to have him talking about her, although she was sure he did.

"There's a gate open." He finally broke the quiet. It was almost completely dark, and she was having trouble seeing him. "Just a small one. Down there," Chloe thought he was pointing, but she couldn't see which direction. "S'rusty."

"Thank you. I'll check as soon as I can." She knew he wasn't happy about the gnomes, likely because it meant he saw less of her. Chloe didn't feel a need to visit Benny for the company of the ghoul.

"'K." There was another shuffle. His voice was more distant now. "Night."

"Have a good night, Benny."

Silence fell again, aside from the light patter of rainfall. The drizzle had made up its mind. Chloe headed for the library, guided by the warm light falling through the windows onto the cold world outside.

"Good evening," Mr. Cruor looked up as she closed the door behind her and put the umbrella in the weird, huge vase shaped like an elephant's foot. "I see it is raining."

"Yes, just started." Chloe headed for her desk. "Sorry to disturb you, but I needed a book, ah!" She held it up. "Trunk wants a two-page essay from me."

"And how are you enjoying being back in school?" He had turned his chair and was sitting back in it, his elbows on the wooden arms, fingers steepled together in front of him.

"I hadn't thought of it as school, when I could help it." Chloe tucked the book carefully into her bag. It wouldn't do to get the century-old text wet. "So, I have been enjoying it. It's like Trunk and I are playing a game, most days."

"Learning should not be painful, Miss Brandt." He rose when she headed for the door and held it open for her as she gathered her umbrella at the ready.

"Well, I'm learning and it's not hurting, so maybe I'm learning that too?" She popped the umbrella out the door, opened it, and stepped into its shelter. "Like having an umbrella means I'm much warmer in the rain."

"Indeed. Good night."

Chloe reached her apartment safely dry and with no more ghoul gossip sessions. Benny wasn't often out in the rain. He must have really missed her. Chloe switched on music, but didn't crank it out of consideration for the gnomes next door, and flopped on her little couch to read and make notes. One thing she'd learned; writing two pages was easy when you had good topics. Keeping it that short was the hard part when you wanted to include more on comparative burial practices.

She hadn't meant to fall asleep on the couch, but Chloe woke with a start. Just as the night before, there had been something. She sat up, rubbing her eyes. She'd left the light on, and her music had paused itself, so the apartment was quiet and visibly empty. She checked the time. Just after midnight. Again.

Chloe got up, turned out the light, and then stood by the window which looked over the parking lot and across to the big house. She pulled aside the blind, just enough to see out, once her eyes had adjusted to the near dark. Chloe kept a nightlight in the bathroom, and the door standing partly open meant there was a dim glow behind her.

A light still shone in the big house, on the second floor. As she watched, another light came on, in one of the small rooms just under the edge of the roof. With the light from those, she could see there were some piles of leaves at the edge of the parking lot. Which was odd. There hadn't been leaves there earlier, and Padraig wouldn't have been raking in the dark. Chloe couldn't see them clearly, and when the larger light in the window went out, she couldn't make out the leaves at all. The light in the highest room moved. She looked, and could see a dim glow in the room, then nothing. It was very strange.

Chloe watched the dark for another moment, then yawned. She would get some sleep and clear leaves in the morning. She'd forgotten, for the moment, the chance of a phone call.

Two hours later, she jolted upright in bed when her phone went off. She scrambled for it, stumbling into the other room.

"'Lo?"

"Fifteen moments, Miss Brandt." Her boss's voice was wide awake as ever.

"Yessir." The line went dead.

Chloe scrambled into clothes. Her black jeans were fine, no holes, and a button-down shirt in a dark purple - almost black - was also acceptable. She wasn't wearing makeup, and her hair went back in a quick French braid to keep it neatly out of the way. Lacing up her boots took the longest, and she didn't even look, she just took her umbrella with her.

At the bottom of the stairs, she ducked around the corner and into the stables. The light was on in the sedan. Mr. Cruor was putting something in the trunk, which he closed, and then he saw her.

"Exemplary time. Miss Brandt. Did you need anything else?"

"Umbrella, notebook, pen?"

"That will do. Shall we?"

He opened the door for her, waited until she was in the car and buckling up, then closed it firmly for her. Chloe had decided she would never get used to that. He used the remote to open the garage door, then pulled out. He always backed into the garage. She didn't know how he managed it, other than long practice.

The light of the car's headlights swung over the wet asphalt, and then...

"Oh dear," Chloe heard herself say.

The big oak had fallen. The piles of leaves she'd seen earlier were the tips of branches reaching into the parking lot from where it had tipped, the roots jutting skyward in the dark beyond them.

"That," Mr. Cruor carefully pulled past the leaves, which didn't reach far enough to block their driveway, "is a tomorrow problem. Also, you have sufficient help to deal with it."

CHAPTER 6
THE LITTLE OLD LADY

"The address is near Eden Park."

Chloe was very glad Mr. Cruor was driving, as it was still raining, the streetlights in the part of town near the cemetery mostly didn't work, and he wasn't using a GPS. She would be terminally lost already. He seemed to know exactly where he was going.

"I don't know why that's important," she admitted. She knew where it was, she thought. It was high on a bluff over the Ohio River. "There's a tower there?"

"Yes, the Ohio River Monument, you've been there?"

"When I was younger," Chloe shrugged in the dark. "The parents thought it was a good place to see the river, and it was interesting to watch the big boats." It had been one of the last family trips with her father, and a cold blustery day. She could remember how pale his face had been, while her mother's and brother's cheeks had been rosy. "I haven't been back."

"No reason to, unless you were in the area for the art museum."

"Not the art museum." Chloe dredged up an even older memory. "To look at butterflies?"

"Ah, yes, the conservatory. The neighborhood is quite the cluster of cultural wealth, which attracts those who patronize such."

"So, she's a rich little old lady." Chloe thought about this. "Which is why they called in outsiders."

"Almost certainly."

"But not for poor little old ladies?"

"Don't feel too badly. The poor ladies are more likely to have family around them and not need to rely on strangers so much. It does happen just … less often."

"I'd never thought about it that way." Chloe leaned back in the soft seat. One thing about heading across the city at this hour of night; there was no traffic. She'd seen about four other vehicles so far.

"And to serve the poor old ladies, the Brotherhood has other partners. You'll meet them soon enough."

"Right then, the police, and others, call on us when something goes bump in the night."

"Yes." He turned into a long, tree-lined driveway which snaked up a steep hillside. They were on the other side of the valley from Belleview's heights. "Unless that something happens to be a falling tree."

Chloe yawned; she couldn't help it. She was not looking forward to any of this.

They came to a stop in front of a big house which was mostly dark. There was another car, and the front door opened. In the wedge of light this spilled out, a dark figure stood waiting on them.

"Let us go and see what there is to see." Mr. Cruor came around to take Chloe's door and she felt ashamed of herself for already having started to open it. This habit was going to take time and thought, and she didn't have much brain to spare at this time of the ni... no, morning.

"That was fast." Detective Murray met them as they came up the steps onto the wide covered porch, which was held up by tall columns, allowing the rain to blow right in on them. Murray wore a ball cap. The rain sparkled in Mr. Cruor's silver hair. Chloe angled her umbrella to try and give him some shelter as well.

"There was no traffic." Mr. Cruor's voice didn't hold a trace of humor. Chloe didn't know how he did it. She couldn't make a joke that deadpan.

Chloe looked around as soon as they all walked into the house. Other than 'bland,' nothing stuck out to her as Detective Murray led them into the kitchen, where his partner was waiting with the stereotypical little old lady.

"Ma'am," Detective Murray spoke first. "These are expert consultants who will need your permission to walk through the house and grounds."

"Just walk? Not search?"

She might be wearing two sets of glasses, one hanging by a bedazzled cord around her neck, the other nestled into her short, curly gray hair, but Chloe thought their little old lady was still sharp as a tack.

"Not search," Mr. Cruor said quietly but firmly. "Just look, we don't need to touch anything."

"I'm too tired to take you," She waved them off. "Murray..."

"Yes, ma'am." The detective led them right back out of the room.

He stopped in the hallway and looked at Mr. Cruor and Chloe's boss just nodded and walked down the hall.

"Sir?" Chloe asked in a very soft voice.

"Yes?" He stopped at the doorway to a sitting room, not

the big formal living room they'd passed on their way in. He wasn't looking at her; he was looking into the room, his eyes moving from one corner to another.

"Is it ok for me to talk?"

"Yes, and I'm sure you have questions."

He looked at her, nodded, and kept going. Chloe hadn't seen any movement in the room, just dimly lit furniture.

"She didn't ask what we were, or who we are."

"No, and likely will not. An educated, rational woman will not like to hear the words ghost, or paranormal, let alone join them with the word hunter. Not in her home."

Mr. Cruor stopped by a closed door and looked back at the detective who'd stayed near the kitchen door.

"Don't worry about prints." The detective waved him on.

Mr. Cruor opened the door, revealing a room completely dark, so dark Chloe had no idea what size it was, let alone its purpose. Mr. Cruor produced his little flashlight with the red bulb from his pocket and shone it into the room.

There was a long table with chairs, and a China hutch. Chloe recognized a formal dining room, and as the light flashed over the far wall, a door leading to the kitchen. Mr. Cruor stepped into the room, headed for that door.

"Sir?"

"No light under the door." He pointed the flashlight at his feet for a second, and she saw what he meant. "Ah, you see," he pulled open the door, and there was another door a few feet away, with light coming under it from the kitchen. "A butler's pantry. Common in a house this size, where catered parties were likely held."

"Or a butler?" Chloe was right behind him as they left the room again.

"Likely not in the era, perhaps hired for a special event, but most likely no servants when the family was in its heyday. A decade earlier, yes. Not by the seventies, though."

There was a guest bathroom and a small bar, and at the back of the house, a sunroom which overlooked a dark garden.

"The moon is rising," Chloe commented, looking through the wall of glass panes.

"We will go out when we've finished the house, and it should be bright enough to make our way." Mr. Cruor walked briskly back up the hall.

As they passed Detective Murray, he fell in behind them. They reached the stairs in the grand foyer, and Mr. Cruor led the way up to the next floor.

"I saw something." Chloe pointed towards an open door at the end of the hall, through which a pale blue light was visible. "Something low to the floor."

"Is there a cat?" Mr. Cruor asked the detective.

"Two of them."

"Then presumably," Mr. Cruor moved more slowly towards the open door. "But always verify, Miss Brandt."

The blue light was from a television on a dresser where it could be watched from the bed. It was clear from the tousled bedding that this is where the little old lady had been sleeping. Now, there were two cats, crouched on the sheets side-by-side, regarding them with wide, dark eyes. One was a gray tabby, the other pure black.

"I think it was the black one..." Chloe looked up at the ceiling. "Or not."

Above the bed was a black stain, like soot or smoke, which moved as they looked at it, then slowly disappeared, leaving a pale popcorn ceiling which looked very normal.

"Is there," Mr. Cruor asked, without turning his head, "an attic access?"

"I assume so, but it hasn't come up."

"Could you please ask?"

Mr. Cruor was standing still as a statue. Chloe realized the cats were also staring up at the ceiling now. She wondered if they had seen it, too. That would explain why cats tended to look at weird blank walls or empty corners, though. Chloe looked around the room.

There was a desk with a closed laptop computer on it. A small table with a magazine and a glass of water stood next to the bed. And on the far wall were double doors. She went towards them. A house like this should have… She pulled them open.

Inside there was a small dressing area with a vanity table and mirrors everywhere. Beyond that, through a doorway with no door, was a huge closet, almost as big as her apartment. Chloe could see motion reflected in the mirrors. One of the cats was walking across the bed, towards her. The other was still, staring at the ceiling, like her boss.

Chloe looked up at the ceiling in the closet. She raised her voice. "I found the attic access."

She could hear Detective Murray's heavy steps on the stairs. The black cat came up to her and sniffed carefully at her legs, then sat down and looked up, not at Chloe, but past her at the hatch on the ceiling.

"Access is in the closet …" Murray's voice from the bedroom door seemed to snap her boss out of his reverie.

"Yes, thank you."

Mr. Cruor joined Chloe, looking at the hatch.

"How do we open it?" she asked. It was a flat, flush

panel and the only way she'd seen it was the seam all the way around.

"There must be, ah!" He had been looking around, and now he reached behind a rack of shirts to pull out a long stick, like a broomhandle. Using this, he pushed up against the panel. There was a click, then it dropped down towards them, along with a bunch of dust and clumps of gray stuff.

Chloe stepped back, as did her boss, until the dustfall had subsided. On the back of the panel was a folded metal ladder, and he reached out and unfolded it until there was a serviceable set of steps, from floor to the very dark hole in the ceiling above them. Mr. Cruor pulled out his flashlight and shone it up into the cavity.

"That's interesting." He moved the light and himself around the ladder, not stepping onto it, peering upwards.

"What is it?" Chloe could see walls, but not much else.

"There appears to be a finished room. In most attics, you'd be looking at rafters and rough-finished wood. I can see a chair back, from this angle."

"I'm going up there," Chloe announced, taking a step onto the ladder. Mr. Cruor didn't argue with her. She couldn't see anything as her head rose above the ladder's top, at first. He'd stopped shining his red light up. Then, a fluorescent tube on the ceiling flickered into life.

"I found the light switch," Mr. Cruor spoke from the level of her ankles.

"I found the spooky part," Chloe answered. She had stopped on the ladder, one hand gripping the very inadequate bar which served as a handrail. "I think this falls into the look, don't touch, sir."

"Come down." His voice had changed, and this was clearly an order. Chloe forced her hand loose from the rail and looked down at her feet, backing slowly down the rungs.

Mr. Cruor stepped up on the ladder when she was clear of it until his top half was out of sight and he was there for a long quiet moment before he came down.

"Detective Murray." He walked back into the other room, Chloe so close on his heels she was almost his shadow. "I do believe this is going to be your case from here."

Murray's eyebrows climbed so high they almost disappeared under his tousled hairline. "You aren't sure?"

"Without touching something we should not, no."

"There's a big stain. A nasty big stain, coming from the luggage under the bed." Chloe shuddered. She didn't tell the detective there was a ghost lying asleep on the bed, half-sunk into it, and that the bed appeared to be right over the bed the little old lady had been trying to sleep in. Mr. Cruor seemed to be in agreement with her; the ghost and the stain were connected.

"There's a bed up there?"

"More of a cot, and a chair, and a little folding TV tray." Mr. Cruor confirmed. "The room does not appear to have been fully finished; it is unpainted, but the walls are drywall. And it was most definitely inhabited."

Chloe had seen that, too, the plate on the tray with its dried remains of something impossible to identify.

"The quilt is old. Older than the house, if this house was built in the 1970s." She added.

Both men looked at her, and she felt her face heating with a blush.

"Care to elaborate?" Murray's voice was encouraging.

"It's the fabric. If some of it was pieced from old material, maybe, but all that I saw was prints that were probably from the 1950s, maybe early sixties. And the color is also that era, the dyes were different..." She floundered. "It's a gut feeling, maybe I'm wrong."

"I don't think you are," Mr. Cruor shook his head. "For one thing, the request for the attic access didn't seem to raise an alarm with the owner. I think you will find," he was addressing Detective Murray, "she had no idea there was a room up there."

"I think there's another access." Chloe blurted.

Both men looked at her, again. She squirmed. "This one wasn't obvious. And it's not the only closet. There's no way to get to the roof, you said," she was looking at her boss, then she turned to Murray. "And she didn't say *her* closet?"

"No, just *the* closet."

"Is there one in the hall?"

The three of them went out of the bedroom, leaving the access door open behind them. Chloe scooped up the black cat as she went. Cats could disturb evidence, too.

A moment later, the third door revealed a spacious linen and cleaning supply closet, with a hatch in the ceiling. This one had a dangling handle, which Detective Murray carefully pulled open to show the same kind of metal ladder.

Mr. Cruor reached into the room as he was standing just outside the door, and flipped on switches, lighting up the closet and the attic above them. Chloe, even standing beside him with only a narrow sliver of a view, could see the rafters. Murray climbed up a few steps.

"Christmas threw up all over," he reported in a dry tone. "Tinsel and fake flower petals everywhere. Totes labeled ornaments..." He backed down the ladder.

"This is what she meant for us to find." Chloe was certain of it.

"We can't read her intentions," Mr. Cruor corrected very

gently. "She may well have subconsciously meant for us to find that other room. She has been a haunted woman, if she knew there was a death just above her head, however many years past..."

"I'll call crime scene." Murray sounded tired. "And if you don't mind..."

"We shall go right away." Mr. Cruor nodded. "No need for our continued assistance, I think."

CHAPTER 7
CURIOSITY AND THE CAT

Chloe looked down into the big golden eyes of the cat she was holding. "Um. What do I do with him?"

"Put him down?" Murray suggested.

"What if he climbs..." Chloe was a little surprised the cat had just curled into her, content to be in her arms.

"I'll keep an eye on him." Murray was surprisingly gentle. "He'll be ok."

Chloe realized the fatherly detective was still comparing her to his young daughter, who would undoubtedly have been very upset by what Chloe had just seen.

"Yes." She bent and put the cat down on the floor. He circled her legs, then walked back towards the bedroom where his tabby compatriot was napping on the unmade bed. Someone had turned on the light in there, too. Chloe hadn't even noticed it.

"Good night, or should I say, good morning." Mr. Cruor held out his hand, and Murray shook it. "We are gone, and have never been here."

"Damn straight." The detective huffed what was almost a laugh.

Chloe followed her boss down into the dark house, and right out the front door. The rain hitting her face was almost a surprise. They hadn't been in the house long, but it had felt like all night, and it should be light outside. She checked her watch. Dawn, for what it was worth on a rain-soaked morning like this, wouldn't come for another three hours.

"Sir?"

"We can talk on the way home. In the warm, dry car." Mr. Cruor had his hand on her elbow, steering her towards the black sedan.

Chloe waited until they were well away from the house. "What happens next?"

"For us? Likely nothing. They will have a team come in, collect evidence, and evaluate what is found."

"What did we find?" Chloe splayed out her hands, pale in the darkness of the car interior. Streetlights flickered overhead as they passed in and out of their lights.

"A ghost, and other than that, it is unclear. The police will puzzle it out. I realize you are curious..."

"Yes, I'm sorry." Chloe slouched back, pushing into the soft leather of the seat. "I should just drop it?"

"Not necessarily, answers are important to you. But remember, you can't assume that what you think is the correct answer, is actually the correct answer."

"Who puts a body in a suitcase? Or locks someone in the attic?" She heard her voice rising as she asked the pressing questions that had been in her head and wanted out.

"Perhaps someone who doesn't want to admit a person

is dead." Mr. Cruor looked in her direction as he stopped for the light. His eyes were large and dark in the dimness. "And perhaps there was someone who wasn't officially supposed to be there, and that was a hiding place."

"Really?" Chloe had been assuming the dead woman had not been up there of her own will. "She looked so young."

"Remember that a ghost's apparent age is not what they were at death."

"Yes." Chloe did remember that her friend Mark looked a little older than she was, but had been an old man when he passed peacefully with much undone research to occupy him for an eon after his body gave out. "So an old lady went up and down that ladder?"

Mr. Cruor surprised her with a chuckle. "Asking the right questions."

"Which can't have answers." Chloe sighed dramatically. "Well, until we get the report."

"Yes, and even then, some will never be answered. We can't ask her."

"Why was that?"

"She wasn't fully awake. Her ghost was not there for us." He drove in silence for a while. "I've seen this before, a spirit bound to a specific person, which would not acknowledge anyone else existed."

"Oh." Chloe contemplated this. "She was haunting the little old lady."

"What did you notice about the suitcase, since you noted the quilt?"

"It was old-fashioned." She closed her eyes and brought it up in her mind. "No plastic. Locking mechanism was chrome, though. Quilt wasn't stained."

"Quite right. The suitcase was of a later era than the quilt. Which, by the way, Detective Murray will ask you about when he sees you next."

"What? Why?"

"Because it wasn't there." Mr. Cruor answered simply. "It was part of the ghost. Likely from the same era as her memory of herself at that age."

"Oh. Oh!" Chloe started to connect things in her head. "So... so she would have been in the house twenty years later when it was built, and that would make her about fortyish?"

"Did you see her face clearly?" Mr. Cruor signaled, and turned into the gates of Belleview, which slid open for the car.

"Not really, just that she was young and probably oriental."

"No," Mr. Cruor shook his head. He'd stopped outside the closed garage doors, and now he opened his door, illuminating his face as he looked at Chloe. "That is an epicanthic fold, sometimes called Mongloid. Down's Syndrome."

He got out, and went to pull the garage door open while Chloe thought about it. If anything, this made it worse. A handicapped child. Hidden from the world, so her family could pretend she didn't exist. She got out of the car.

"Go get some sleep if you can," Mr. Cruor patted her shoulder. "Keep this in mind, that Down's Syndrome often affects the heart, and many people who live with it do not live long lives."

"She died in her sleep, under the quilt someone made for her with love and she loved them. That's why she had it and I could see all the details and even colors." Chloe took a deep breath. "Yeah, I think I'll go make a cup of sleepy tea."

"Good." Mr Cruor closed the car door and pulled forward.

Chloe headed for her stairs and paid no attention to the soft cold rain.

Chloe slept until noon. She wasn't entirely sure when she'd finally crawled into bed, but with the blinds down and curtains drawn, her apartment was nicely dark. Kettle on, she checked for messages from her boss and found nothing. There were four from Padraig. She scrolled through them, winced, and sent a message to Mr. Cruor.

Chloe dressed for heavy outdoor work while she steeped her tea, then transferred that to a travel mug. She wasn't going to have a quiet day at home.

"Chloe?" Her boss met her as she opened the library door. "Do you know what has Padraig so wound up?"

"No, just that he wanted us to meet him at the fallen tree." Chloe had almost forgotten it, in the urgency of their police business. "It's not raining at the moment."

"I'll change shoes and be right along." Her boss retreated, and Chloe headed for the tree. The oak had fallen into the lawn, with topmost branches reaching all the way to the drive, but not blocking it, as they'd been able to skirt past them in the car the night before. The bigger branches seemed to have broken on impact when it came down, giving it a weirdly flattened effect, except where the roots had come up. They formed a huge disc of still-green turf as Chloe walked around the tree's branches and towards it. Twisted roots thrust outward like gnarled tentacles. Padraig appeared with a rustle of dead oak leaves.

"Wasn't expecting this."

"Neither was I," Chloe agreed. "Sorry I wasn't available earlier, we were gone half the night."

He grunted, with a hand wave. "It's not urgent, just…"

Mr. Cruor, wearing appropriate sturdy half-boots, came up just then. "You are concerned."

"Yeah. Above my paygrade, this." Padraig gestured towards the roots.

They followed him around and to the edge of the muddy crater the upheaval had left.

Padraig pointed. Not into the crater, but at the rough center of the roots.

Chloe could see it. There really was only one thing shaped like that, even if she couldn't see both eye sockets from this angle, and the lower jawbone was missing. She looked down into the mud, and could see more bones as she focused on the shapes in the dark earth. They were not white.

"Well, then." Mr. Cruor stroked his chin. "That is interesting."

"Me'n t'boys were talking." Padraig's accent was all over the place when he was upset, Chloe had learned, "If'n we cut the trunk the roots should just… settle back in place."

"And then we pretend we never saw this?" Mr. Cruor raised an eyebrow.

"Yeh." The gnome kicked a clod of mud, which stuck to the toe of his battered brown boot.

"Sir, is it possible the tree grew into a grave?"

"Not only possible, Miss Brandt, but likely. In addition, during the much earlier era of Belleview, there were some, ah, alternative burials made."

"Like the casket filled with oil." Chloe had vivid memories of that incident, and not just because it hadn't been that long ago they'd dealt with oil animated by a spirit.

"Yes. Among others. You have been reading…"

"I have." Chloe had been assigned more than one book on the practices of peoples around the world regarding death and disposal of bodies. "So we should check the map and then, yes, cut the tree?"

"I will leave it in your capable hands, Miss Brandt, Padraig." Mr. Cruor turned and walked back towards the house.

"Right, then." Chloe looked at the mass of branches, which now included the original fallen one. "Start cleaning up the smaller stuff, working towards the trunk?"

"Yeah," Padraig pushed his red cap back a bit and scratched his forehead. "Me'n t'boys will get on it. You push the papers."

"That is my job," Chloe sighed. Right about now wading into this mess with a saw sounded much more appealing. She could see movement of the dead leaves which marked other gnomes hard at work already. They had been listening in, it seemed. She raised her voice slightly. "I'll talk to Mr. Cruor about hiring a big woodchipper. At least we'll have lots of mulch for the gardens."

"True that." Padraig perked up a little. "Woodchipper, eh?"

"Yes. Which you will use cautiously." She gave him her best stern look.

He grinned at her. It wasn't very effective. Chloe would have to keep working on it.

"I'll be back," she promised. "To check in, and hopefully answer why there's a body under the oak."

"Right." He reached into a cluster of branches and pulled out a bow saw. "Back to work."

The crunch of car tires on the drive got her attention, and she turned to see a car carefully maneuvering past the tree. Chloe started walking towards the parking lot, texting her boss rapidly as she went. She didn't need to send more than 'visitor incoming' before she could put the phone away and try to see who it was.

She had reached the edge of the asphalt when the car pulled to a halt at the side of the house by the library door. She was surprised when a very tired-looking Detective Murray climbed slowly out of the driver's side door.

"Hello," Chloe called.

He turned and looked at her. "Is Cruor in?"

"Yes," Chloe was walking fast, without breaking into a run, trying to reach him quickly. "He had just gone back in a few minutes ago. That tree fell down last night."

"It's a big one," Murray looked over her shoulder. "I have something for you."

Chloe remembered what Mr. Cruor had said about the quilt, and felt her stomach tighten with anticipation. Instead, Murray opened the passenger door and pulled out a small carrier.

"Here." He pushed it at her. "You were worried about it."

Chloe took the carrier reflexively. It was heavy. She lifted it to see what was in it, and the big gold eyes of the black cat peered at her. There was a loud cry of protest from inside the carrier.

Murray flinched. "Thing screamed at me the whole way here. I'm a dog person."

"Oh. I... um," Chloe wasn't sure what to say.

"My partner took the other one home. Don't know what you know, but it will be a while before anyone could take care of them, and he didn't want 'em to go to the pound."

"Right," Chloe was figuring it out. "Happy to foster him."

There was another shriek from the carrier. Both of them winced.

"I'm going to take him to my place where he can be still and adjust." Chloe hurried away.

Behind her, she heard her boss greeting the detective.

CHAPTER 8
SKY AND TREES

Chloe had intended to go straight to Trunk, and pore over the troll's trove of maps. Now, she realized she was going to have to come up with food, litter, and supplies for a cat. She put the carrier in her bathroom, provided a small amount of water in a bowl, and opened the carrier door, before backing slowly out and closing the door. The black cat was hunkered down in the back of the carrier, his ears pressed flat back against his head.

Having done all she could, because she didn't have tuna on hand... She didn't eat tuna! Chloe lamented as she hurried back down the stairs. Food was less important than litter, though. Nobody wanted the cat to have an accident on the floor. Not her, not the cat, certainly not her landlord and boss. Although he didn't seem to mind pets, perhaps because so far her only pet was a hog-nosed snake who lived in a big terrarium. No mess, there.

Detective Murray seemed to be in the library with her boss, or at least neither man was in sight while the detective's car was still there. Chloe opened the garage and got into the Abomination. For once, she was really grateful for having wheels of her own. She could run her errand and return fairly quickly.

It still took her over an hour by the time she'd traveled to the closest big store, gotten supplies, and then returned home. She headed for her apartment first, but could see that the Detective had already gone. She guessed he hadn't been home and to bed since sometime yesterday or even the day before. Chloe hoped he could get some rest. She assembled the small temporary litter tray before opening her bathroom door. There was no room in there for the proper covered litter box she'd bought, so an aluminum cake pan with a bit of litter would have to do.

She opened the door, and saw the cat sitting on top of the toilet seat, which she'd left closed for safety. He stared at her.

"I have food," Chloe informed him. "And I'm going to put this in the tub, try not to make a big mess, please?" She put the tray down. He didn't move anything other than his head, watching her. At least he wasn't trying to run away or hide.

Half expecting him to try rushing the door now, she slipped through it quickly, closing it securely, then returned with a small bowl of gushy food. This got a reaction, as he lifted his head, nose twitching.

"Hungry, huh? I'm not surprised." She put it down by the water bowl. "I'll leave the carrier. I see someone put a towel in there to keep you warm and soft." She held out a hand, slowly, towards him. He sniffed her fingers, but then looked towards the food bowl. "I'll come check on you later. I wonder what your name is?"

She hadn't thought to ask Detective Murray, although

from how he'd acted, he might not know. If she saw his partner again, though, she could ask him.

"Right. Sorry I'm closing you in, but it's for your own good." She backed out of the door, and as she closed it, saw him jump down towards the food bowl.

Hopeful that he'd warm back up to her with some time, Chloe headed for the big house. This time she really needed to have that chat with Trunk. Surely the day would start to slow down, now?

Mr. Cruor was sitting at his desk in the library, but he was talking on the phone, so Chloe did her best to close the door behind her silently. She intended to slip past him and head down to talk to Trunk, but her boss turned slightly and held up one finger to signal her to wait for him.

She sat at the table, sighed, and reached for her travel mug, which had somehow ended up in here. She didn't even remember where she'd left it that... no, it hadn't been morning. Afternoon. She checked the time. Getting on towards evening at this point. She didn't have a lot of daylight left. The body in the tree had been there for a very long time, and it would take the gnomes time to deal with the branches and she hadn't arranged for a woodchipper yet ... Chloe folded her arms on the table and put her head down on them.

"Are you well, Miss Brandt?"

Mr. Cruor sounded concerned. Chloe sat up straight. "Yes, just ... it's a lot. Did Detective Murray tell you about the cat?"

"No, he did not." Mr. Cruor sat at the table opposite her. "What about it?"

"He brought it to me. He didn't say they arrested the little old lady, but that the cat needed to be looked after for an indefinite amount of time, and his partner took the other cat."

"They did arrest her. I would have expected a rapid release on bond, so it is very interesting they fostered out her pets."

"I didn't even think that through." Chloe yawned. "Sorry, anyway I went and got cat things. The detective didn't seem like he wanted to talk to me."

"He confirmed to me that a body had been found, and an arrest had been made. I'm afraid I don't have more details for you."

Chloe shrugged. "I have to learn to live with mysteries. I also need to arrange for a big woodchipper. Do we have someone we call...?"

"I'll take care of that. You need to confer with Trunk."

"Yes, I do." Chloe agreed fervently. "That's a mystery I'd like to lay to rest as soon as possible."

"Understandable, however..." He paused, uncharacteristically, looking at her with slightly narrowed eyes. "There is something else."

"Oh no," Chloe groaned. "No, sorry, it's all part of the job, isn't it?"

"I am afraid so." Mr. Cruor gave her a crooked smile. "There are often long periods of boredom where I catch up on my reading, so you have that to look forward to."

"It's a myth," Chloe smiled back at him. "What is it now?"

"John called. Something came up on his radar down there, and he wants me to come take a look. Which means you are coming along, as well. He did say there were kittens who love to play."

Chloe laughed. "I haven't gone down there because that's a long drive to make by myself."

"You should consider adopting a kitten."

She blinked at him. "What? I just got handed a cat."

"Cats do better in pairs. They can keep one another company. This one had a friend, possibly a litter mate, and now he is alone."

"Oh." Chloe thought about this. "Well, since we have to go down there anyway, and I was just given a carrier, which conveniently smells like the cat I just got ... Augh. Oh, and are you ok with pets in the apartment?"

He chuckled. "We will go down tomorrow, likely, unless something else crops up here."

"Another body," she grumbled. "Please tell me we've not done any sky burials."

"Not in some time. There are hygiene laws."

Chloe felt her jaw drop open.

Her boss looked at his watch. "You need to talk to Trunk. I need to make calls before close of business to get that chipper."

"We can talk about sky burials on the way to John's." Chloe wasn't sure if she was making a threat or a promise. She got up and headed for the basement and Trunk's lair.

Trunk had never rearranged his living room, or whatever the big open space was, after the initial class where he was teaching Chloe the history of Belleview. The comfy couch, pillows, and ottoman centered in the room were always ready for her, and he welcomed her any time. The walls he'd used for his presentations remained an ever-changing landscape of letters, photos, newspaper clippings, and all interconnected between these were colorful strings and yarns pinned and webbed to show the way history progressed. Messy, sometimes, but there were connections. Chloe shouted a greeting to the empty room, then wandered over to see what was new. She'd encouraged Trunk to write a book, if only to record everything in one place, and he'd dived into that project with enthusiasm. She sometimes wished she could get the troll and her ghost friend Mark in the same place, but there were reasons that was impossible.

"Chloe!" Trunk emerged from one of the big iron-bound doors. "How goes?"

"I need to find out if there's a grave somewhere very specific." Chloe told him. "I'm tired, by the way, and I have a cat? So that's nice. And I have a body under a tree. Well. It was under a tree, now it's kinda up but also down and how are you doing?"

Trunk's eyes got as wide as she'd ever seen those gravelly crevasses on his face open. His mouth hung open slightly.

"Shall I start at the beginning?" she asked, trying not to smile at his obvious bemusement.

"Please. There's a body? In a tree?"

"More like in the tree roots. Don't know when you were last outside?" Chloe knew the troll rarely ventured out these days. Too many ways for him to be seen.

"Been a while," he admitted. "Which tree?"

"The big old oak. There's a skull about in the middle of the roots. It fell over; roots are like so," she looped her arms and bent backwards, miming how the tree had fallen. As she straightened up, she continued, "Mr. Cruor thinks it may have been an alternative burial?"

"Ah," the troll nodded, his joints crunching a little. "So we need the private map. Old Mr. Underwood kep' it. After his time," Trunk spread his hands in an eloquent gesture that meant something like 'who can tell?' "But I'll get his map. If there's a body on it, then you know."

Chloe plopped onto the couch, wondering what happened if there wasn't supposed to be a body under the oak tree. She was fairly sure there wasn't a ghost attached to it, which was a pity, because you could ask questions. If the person was just dead, there was no way to get any answers. Like the woman in the attic. She might never know the answers there. Chloe stared at the ceiling, with its dark exposed beams. The skeleton of the big house.

Trunk re-emerged from wherever he kept the archives, carrying big rolls of paper. "Don't know where we'll put these …" he was looking around like an empty space on the walls would appear.

"On the floor?" Chloe suggested. There was no table, and given Trunk's affinity for clutter, she was a little afraid to suggest he get one.

"Oh, that will work. Hand me a cushion."

She handed him cushions, then her own hand, to use for weighting down the long-coiled paper which really wanted to stay curled up. Chloe peered down at the corner she was holding. "Um. Can you read this?"

"Yes, it's Spencerian."

He was squatting on the floor next to the map, now. "There's the house."

Chloe moved a cushion to hold the corner, taking its place closer to the part she was interested in. "What is Spencer, in this context?"

"A style of calligraphy. I can't even," he held up one of his vast chunky hands. "But it's rather elegant."

"And faded." Chloe pulled the little flashlight she always carried out of her pocket and spotlighted the house. "Stables there, so," She hovered a finger over the map, she'd learned that touching the old paper could have bad effects, "About here. Are the ruffly circles trees?"

"Quite right." He laboriously bent, squinting. "No graves. That would have been planted as a screen from the horses... flies, you know. No windowscreens back then, long before air conditioning. Open windows all summer and the flies..." He shook his head. "Older map, then."

Chloe let go of her corner, then helped rearrange cushions as he put away one and unrolled another map.

"What if," she verbalized her concern, "it's not on these?"

"Well, that tree has been growing since long before Old Underwood was gone, so if a body was buried ... when it was planted, perhaps?"

Chloe contemplated this. One of the books had mentioned people wanting a tree planted over them, but it was a more modern take on burial practices. Connecting with nature, and all that.

"Here," Trunk pointed with a stubby forefinger. "Ah, good, there is a notation."

In tiny, crabbed handwriting, someone had scrawled a sigil, so small Chloe couldn't make it out.

"What does it mean?"

"It's in the log book." He chuckled. "Not that kind of log, even if there was a tree."

Chloe giggled. Trunk made the worst jokes, but they always got her to laugh. Together they got the map rolled up again, and Trunk went after the book. Book HK, page 76. That's what the tiny inscription read, he'd told her.

The book was hand-bound, not uncommon, Trunk had told her, for any book older than the Victorian Era and the Industrial Revolution really taking off. He'd digressed into when that had really started, but Chloe didn't remember all of it. Now, he opened the book carefully and stepped back to let her nimble fingers work the pages gently to the proper entry. Paper had been chosen more for cost than archival quality, if they had even known what factors to look for, there. Now, it was yellowed and very brittle.

"Here," Chloe peered at the handwritten page number. "I think."

"Aye," Trunk agreed, leaning in from the other side. He smelled of moss.

"There are a lot of them." Chloe looked at the page in dismay. There were at least twenty entries on it.

"All from one month in 1861." Trunk hovered his finger over the page, slowly working down it line by line. "Oh. This one."

Chloe read the name out loud. "Dolores Underwood."

"No grave site allocated." Trunk poked at the column where there should have been a number.

"Wait. Underwood?" Chloe connected the dots. "As in, Elias Underwood, the groundskeeper?"

"He'd have been an assistant, then. Likely couldn't afford to put her in a proper site."

"So, who *was* she?" Chloe looked at the partially-filled-out line on the page.

"His wife, I believe." Trunk shook his head. "Story was she died in childbirth. He never remarried. He'd have wanted her close by to him, though."

"And the child?" Chloe was struck by the pathos of the idea. Had Old Underwood worked at the cemetery to his dying day to remain close to his wife's final resting place?

"Dunno, but likely with her. He had no children to carry on his work."

Chloe remembered that, after Underwood's death, had come what Trunk termed the dark years of Belleview, as the upheaval of World Wars and their aftermath led slowly to the deterioration of the cemetery and its gardens. Chloe took a step back, and let out her breath slowly. It was a tragic story, and one she knew from her research was all too common in the world where modern medicine wasn't available, even now.

"This means we can leave her to rest in peace."

Trunk, carefully closing the book, nodded. "He must have planted the oak as a marker for her, since he couldn't have put a stone up for them."

"I wonder..." Chloe wrinkled her nose in thought. "I have an idea about that."

Then she shook her head and returned to the present. "Thank you, Trunk. That was most helpful. I need to go see if there's any light left in the day, and talk to the gnomes."

"Most welcome. I had always wondered, myself." He carried the book carefully away, and Chloe ran up the stairs.

She found that there was perhaps another hour of light remaining. Mr. Cruor was not in the library, so she passed right through it and went out to find Padraig. There was a tall stack of leafy branches, and she could see that they had begun working inward, breaking the tree down as they went. Chloe wondered if she should whistle a tune or something as she approached to give the shyer gnomes a chance to hide. Padraig came out across the lawn to meet her, a saw carried over his shoulder.

"How is it going?" Chloe asked. "It looks like you've all made a lot of progress."

"Aye," Padraig turned and pointed. "Cleared the road, and getting it back to the bigguns."

She guessed he meant the larger branches.

"I found out the body is supposed to be there." She told him. "And I have an idea, but I'd need your help."

He looked up at her, his eyebrows raised to the brim of his cap.

"What if we cut the trunk so that, I don't know," She held her hand up over her head, "That much? Was sticking up?"

"Could do." He looked towards the main trunk. "Might have to cut a branch flush, no reason we can't."

"And then? Can we carve it?" Chloe asked. "I've seen sculptures made of tree trunks. It seemed like a way to mark her grave, and her child's."

"Ah, then." He fell silent for a moment, tugging on his beard. Chloe had seen him do this before when he was busy thinking. "A woman and child?"

"Elias Underwood's wife and only child," Chloe elaborated. "Her name was Dolores."

"Well, then." Padraig's voice was very soft. Chloe didn't think he was old enough to have known Underwood, but then again, she wasn't about to ask. "Aye. We could do that. He was a friend to the clan."

"Thank you, Padraig." Chloe stood there staring at the tree for a long moment.

"We'll do that cut in the morning," he said after a period of silence. "Set the trunk back up and rest her."

"If it's safe." Chloe cautioned him.

"Oh, that we can do w'no problem." Padraig shrugged. "Easier than trying to do it flush."

"Good," Chloe was going to trust he knew what he was doing. "What are we going to do with all this wood? Most of this is going to be too big to mulch. Also, Mr. Cruor was going to arrange a woodchipper."

"Firewood." Padraig answered her briefly. "No stoves in the apartment, but t'house has fireplaces. We'll cut n'stack it neat-like."

"That works, then." Chloe took a deep breath. "And I don't know how much I'll be around to help."

"You don't worry about that." He looked up at her again, his eyes narrowed so his bushy gray brows almost hid them. "I'm yer right-hand-man, you do what spooky stuff y'gotta."

Chloe smiled at him. "Thank you, Padraig. I don't know what I'd do without you."

To her surprise, he got very pink in the cheeks and nose, and stomped off, grumbling audibly but not coherently.

CHAPTER 9
ROAD TRIP

"Della has packed us a lunch, and we will have to take the, er, Abomination." Mr. Cruor announced when Chloe had barely taken a sip from her morning tea.

"Oh, Della lunch..." She froze, her cup in midair. "We have to do *what* now?"

"John told me when he called that he'll be taking us up a road which is in poor repair, and unpaved for sections. He warned me that the town car was not going to make it, and as he said 'it's too pretty to die like that.' so I should come down in the Abomination."

"And added a dig about surviving my driving, probably," Chloe grumbled, then drank more tea.

"You have improved greatly." Mr. Cruor sipped some of his own tea. "Will the, ah, vehicle make the trip?"

"I don't know? If John thinks it will, likely?" Chloe shrugged and ate more of her Welsh Cakes. Della really had gone all out on making sure they were sustained for their expedition into the wilds of Kentucky. Chloe had realized the skeletal housekeeper got anxious when Mr. Cruor, and now by extension, Chloe herself, left Belleview for any length of time.

"We shall have faith, then. What will you need to do before we leave?"

Chloe thought about it. "I should dress like I'm going to be working outdoors, it sounds like, so I'll change. I want to check in with Padraig. They will be standing the stump up today, so poor Mrs. Underwood isn't exposed to the elements any longer."

She had briefed him the night before on what she had learned about the body.

"So, perhaps an hour before we depart." He checked his watch. "The weather report indicates there is a chance of rain."

Chloe sighed loudly. "I'll pack my umbrella."

"It could be snow," he admonished gently with a hint of a smile.

"Not if I'm driving, it can't," Chloe shot back. She finished off the buttery Welsh Cake, which had been jammed full of currants. "I'll meet you in an hour."

Before an hour had passed, Chloe had loaded her gear into the Land Rover. There was enough space in the back to hold what she deemed might be necessary. Things like a spade, a bucket, and pruning shears, were in there from her last trip to Eloise, who had sent her home with cuttings and instructions on how to responsibly rustle roses or other remnants from roadsides where old farmhouses had once stood - or still did, abandoned and decaying. Chloe hadn't quite brought herself to the point where she'd risk that, but the tools remained available.

The picnic basket, which was quite substantial, went on the back seat. Chloe had packed a very small overnight bag, or alternatively, emergency pants, and tucked that down below the seat. She was setting up her phone in its clamp-stand on the dashboard to serve as GPS when Mr. Cruor appeared. He was wearing a sweater, a tweed jacket, and canvas pants with cargo pockets, which made Chloe blink at him. He smiled.

"No offense, sir, but you look like you're going on safari or something," she told him as he climbed into the passenger seat. "You could drive, you know."

"I have worn this on safari, I think you need practice, and besides, it really does behave better with your hand on the wheel."

Chloe turned the key partway, counted to two under her breath, then finished turning it. The engine started with its rattling roar. "I don't know what you mean," she responded to him in her primmest tone.

She looked at the gas gauge. "I'm going to fill up before we get on the highway," she said as she started to pull out of the parking lot. Since it wasn't raining right then, she'd opted to pull out of the garage before loading. They needed more light in the garage, in her opinion.

"This seems prudent," her boss settled back.

Chloe pulled into the gas station at the foot of the hill. She didn't think the student boy would be behind the counter at this hour, but to her surprise, he was. She put her beverage on the counter. "Don't you ever go home?"

He yawned. "Yeah, but Donny called in before my shift was over and there's no coverage."

"Ouch," Chloe sympathized. "Thanks," as he gave her back her change. "Well, I don't know if it's better to be dead so you can study, or busy so the time passes. Whichever, I hope you get it."

"Dead," he responded with fervor and wide dark eyes behind the mop of dark curls. "I have an exam tomorrow."

"Luck!" Chloe made the bells on the door bounce and tinkle as she left to climb back into the truck.

"What is that?" Mr. Cruor pulled the drink out of the holder to see it. "Liquid Death?"

"It's an energy drink, one that works for me." Chloe was focused on getting back on the road. "Lots of vitamins, not too much caffeine."

"Interesting." He replaced it. "I will not report back to Della."

Chloe laughed. "It's a road trip, certain things are requirements. Snacks, drinks…"

"Loud music?" Mr. Cruor sounded amused.

"Well, no, I don't want to inflict my music on you, sir."

"Then we can talk," he offered.

However, he settled back in his seat and fell silent while Chloe reached the more heavily trafficked area, then got on the interstate. Driving through half the city was better than all of it, but it wasn't until they were over the Ohio River bridge and well into Kentucky that he spoke again.

"You asked about sky burials."

Chloe remembered that conversation with an effort. The last day had been very eventful. "Yes, and you said there had been some at Belleview?"

"Not in the traditional sense, necessarily." She passed a semi, and he waited until she was back in her lane. "The bodies were exposed to the elements, not on a platform, but in a specialized mausoleum."

"Wouldn't that stink?" Chloe made a face.

"Yes, but this was in the early days, and it was as far from any public as possible."

"So why?"

"To have only bones remaining for placement in a crypt. A body takes up far more space than a bundle of dry bones.

This was once, and possibly historically before written records, a very common method of dealing with the dead."

"I know from the books that burial is, well, it's changed over the history of humanity."

"Indeed. Burials were almost certainly reserved for the very important, be they royalty of some definition in a tribe, or high religious figures. There's little way of telling for certain who these honored dead were in life, but we can make assumptions from what was buried with them, or how they were buried."

"Like the bog bodies." Now, those had creeped Chloe out when she'd read about them, and then looked up photos on the internet. "Human sacrifice, ugh."

"Mmm." Mr. Cruor made a noise.

"They were murdered?" She wasn't sure what he'd meant.

"Yes." He didn't elaborate. "Some nomadic peoples carried their dead with them, rather than leave them in fixed gravesites, which was their way of honoring them."

"I can kind of understand that," Chloe moved over a lane, as their exit was coming in just a couple of miles. "I mean, if I didn't know ghosts, it would seem weird, but the ghosts would come along with their bones, and be with their people."

"So, wait, when burials were only for the high muckety-mucks, what about their ghosts?"

"We don't know," Mr. Cruor responded. "There's no way to know, not that far back in history. Moving up in time a few thousand years, we know the cities in Europe, pressed sorely for space, utilized extensive catacombs and crypts under the surface dwellings."

"I do not ever want to visit those." Chloe signaled her turn. "I can only imagine how many ghosts."

"And other things, yes. They are not safe for the Brotherhood, and are handled by a specialist sector."

Chloe glanced at her directions, then took the left turn indicated. There wasn't a town right at this exit, and they were driving through farmland within a mile of leaving the interstate.

"Did John give you any hints about what we're going to be doing today, other than going off the beaten track?" Chloe looked around. They were driving almost due east, now, having plunged south well into Kentucky. She knew that ahead of them lay the backbone of the Appalachian mountain range, ancient and worn to a nub, but still mountains.

"Since he has no sensitivity, he couldn't say for certain. However, there was a disturbance and someone whose word he trusts said it was due to spirits."

"So, ghosts."

"Not necessarily," her boss shook his head. "You've been talking to Eloise about elementals."

"Earth spirits?" Chloe nodded. "I don't know if I can see those, though, I mean, it's really hard to tell them apart from wind if I can."

"This is true, and they are difficult as they don't communicate, per se." He paused, and she slowed as they came into a small town, graying and decrepit. There were few vehicles on the road, but the speed limit dropped as the road entered town. "However, those sensitive to them say they can read them, in a manner like body language, which hints at disturbances unseen and can lead them to an origin."

"That could be useful." Chloe sped back up as they got to the other side of the town and she was allowed. "But Eloise makes it sound like herding cats."

He chuckled. "Speaking of cats, how is the cat doing?"

"Cat is exploring the bathroom and making noises about wanting out." Chloe had managed to keep him in, when she'd checked his water and given gushy food that morning. "I don't want him exploring the whole place until I'm able to be there with him."

"Sensible."

"Hopefully tomorrow?" Chloe shrugged.

"You did bring an overnight bag?" Her boss had put a bag of his own on the seat behind him.

"Yes." Chloe slowed again. They were coming into another tiny town. "I was hoping not to need it. For one thing, I haven't seen any hotels."

"It is always best to be prepared," Mr. Cruor pointed. "Shall we stop at the gas station and have a bio break?"

"Yes," Chloe agreed, and pulled into the parking lot.

There was a single restroom, with a key taped to a stick, so they took turns. Chloe browsed the store for something to buy in exchange for their bathroom use while her boss was in the necessary. Although there were some baked goods arranged on the scratched glass counter, she didn't see any labels on them and decided to take a pass. A packet of chips in hand, she paid and left, to wait in the Abomination. The greasy-haired woman with the blank eyes behind the counter had given Chloe a bad feeling.

Mr. Cruor rejoined her, a bottle of water in hand.

"Ready?" he asked as he buckled in.

"So ready." Chloe got the Land Rover started. "Something... off, there."

"Sadly, this area is poor, drug-addicted, and so backwards they joke the end of the world will arrive twenty years after it has happened elsewhere." He glanced out the side window at the rundown houses. None of them appeared to have been painted in a generation, if not longer. A few had mowed yards. More had a tangle of weeds and bare dirt.

"That is sad. What happened?"

"This area has always been rural, but the few manufacturing jobs moved out of the country, collapsing what little industry supported the area. Agriculture has moved towards a corporate, large-scale model, which displaced families and lost more jobs as automation replaced farmers. What remains is people too poor or too proud to move to where work is. And the drug trade. Which is definitely not safe nor healthy."

"Yeah." Chloe hadn't seen much of that. Her parents had sheltered her, and by the time she'd been in high school she'd known better than to go the zombie route.

"It started as far back as Prohibition, so more than a century. It has become traditional now: alcohol, then drugs, and you can see the effect."

Chloe shivered, her eyes on the road. No wonder it had given her the heebie-jeebies. It was like one massive ghost of a town had lain over everything back there. A big dark blanket, blocking out the light and hope.

"It's so pretty, though, once you get into the country."

"It is very green. Reminds me strongly of Ireland," Mr. Cruor agreed. "And there is a country which is interesting to visit."

"I can't imagine finding the time to travel," Chloe shook her head. "Ever since you moved me to... doing this. There has been one thing after another."

"Which means that my timing was good. I need your help, Miss Brandt. I know you have doubts of your abilities, however, I am no longer young, and I can see a situation arising which would require me to be in two places at once." He turned his head and gave her a crooked smile. "Which no, I cannot do. So for those times, I must have you able to speak for me, and in due time, to have the experience to bring your own authority to bear."

Chloe took a long, deep breath. "Yes, sir. I'm not certain that will come, but I'll keep trying my best. It's good I can be a helper."

The GPS interrupted them, informing her that there was a turn coming up. She paid more attention to the road. They turned off onto a one-lane, but paved, road, and then into a driveway that led them down a tree-lined gravel drive for a while. The trees opened up to reveal a low brick ranch house. Off to one side stood a big white barn with a red roof.

Chloe pulled the Abomination up next to John's car and parked. By the time she had reminded herself to wait on Mr. Cruor, John was opening her door.

"Hello! You didn't even have to call and ask for help!"

Chloe stuck the tip of her tongue out at him. "We managed just fine!"

CHAPTER 10
WEEPING BRIDE CREEK

"And to reward your driving skills, you get to meet kittens." John stepped away from the Land Rover's door. "At least I don't have to lift this thing off and then back on to close it for you."

Mr. Cruor, coming around to greet him, chuckled. "It is the Abomination, not the antichrist."

"I'm glad to see you surviving and cheerful after your experience this morning, Cruor."

They shook hands.

"I'm right here," Chloe pointed out.

"That you are," John agreed. "Come on, they are waiting. See?"

He pointed at the big glass picture window, and there, lined up along the back of a sofa were four kittens and a larger cat Chloe assumed to be their mother.

"Oh, they are so cute!" She fluttered her fingers at them.

"Killers," John growled as he walked past her. "Monsters with blades on their feet."

All of them got up and ran along the sofa, tumbling over one another, as John moved towards the door.

Chloe laughed. "I can see they are unloved and neglected."

Once inside, the kittens all stopped in their tracks as soon as they saw Chloe behind John. Poised, with big eyes, they stood as she stepped aside for Mr. Cruor. The mother cat, a tortoiseshell with half her face bright orange and a pair of white mittens, strolled past her progeny and stropped John's pantlegs before calmly looking up at Chloe and her boss. This seemed to break the spell of uncertainty, and the kittens charged ahead, straight for John and up the leg of his jeans.

He pulled them off as they climbed as high as his waist, handing them to Chloe as he did so.

"Here, it's dangerous out there." The first kitten to the top was a gray tabby, which Chloe took in both hands. "You shouldn't go alone." The second kitten was orange-and-white. "Take this." Chloe, having had both hands full of kittens already, put the tabby on her shoulder and accepted the little tortie.

"You look like your mother," Chloe cooed at this kitten, while John handed the fourth and final to Mr. Cruor.

"Won't leave you unarmed, sir. Can I get you anything to drink? Bathroom is first door on the right in the hall."

Mr. Cruor placed the bright orange tabby on Chloe's other shoulder, solemnly. "I will return..."

He disappeared into the hall.

"Welcome to my humble abode. Actually, it was my parents' and I inherited it. Which means it's too big for me and I rattle around it like a Mexican jumping bean."

Chloe, having a third kitten climbing her shirt to join its siblings on her shoulders, looked around. "It is nice, though."

"Messy, since I rarely have guests and have a houseful of murdermittens. As you may be feeling."

"They are sharp, yes, but how else could they climb so well?" She kissed the tortie on its soft little head. "They are too cute to be mad at them."

"You don't live with them. Glass of water?"

"Yes, please." Chloe followed him, moving slowly because the kittens dug in when she made any sharp movements. The kitchen was big, and laid out well. She could see there was a pass through to a dining room, and it was separated from the living room by a nice, solid wall.

"Mom designed the house." John handed her a glass of water he'd filled from the spigot on the refrigerator door. "She didn't want smells everywhere, so none of that newfangled open concept. Also, there's a summer kitchen out there," he waved in the general direction of the rear of the house. "So she wasn't heating the whole house while she was canning. Kept a big garden every year of her life, even the last one when it was just me doing what she told me."

"I'm sorry for your loss." Chloe was trying to keep a kitten from leaping between her shoulder and the kitchen island.

"Eh. It's life, they weren't young when they had me - I'm tail-end John Charlie of six - and Mom was missing Dad pretty bad those last two years."

Chloe drank, set her glass down, and set the persistent gray tabby down on the floor. "Mom missed Dad terribly when he was gone, but she said she had us to keep her mind off it."

John cocked his head. "You're young to have lost your Dad."

"I'm twenty," she replied defensively, then sighed, letting it go. "But I was only fifteen when he died. Cancer."

"I'm sorry. Now, we're even. Let's go see if the bossman wants anything."

They found Mr. Cruor sitting upright in a leather armchair, with the mother cat on his lap, her eyes squeezed almost closed in pleasure while he patted her.

"Can I get you tea?" John asked.

"No, thank you," Mr. Cruor responded. The gray tabby kitten launched itself up his leg. He caught it gently and held it up in his hand, looking into the big green eyes. "You are an adventurer."

"He's trouble." John took the kitten and held it with its belly up, tickling the soft pale fur with his fingers.

"And you called us here for trouble." Mr. Cruor continued to slowly pet the mother cat, who seemed to be asleep.

"Yes," John frowned. "And I can't even tell you for certain what it is about."

"What were you told? Not what you know, I can see there are precious few facts which satisfy you in this case."

"That's the thing, it feels like some story made up for sensationalism and possibly to appeal to the internet." He nodded at Chloe, who had sat on the sofa and was playing with the one kitten who hadn't yet fallen asleep on her. John put the gray tabby kitten down next to her and paced around the living room while he talked.

"And yet something made you take it seriously enough to call me." Mr. Cruor had folded his hands over the sleeping cat and was leaning back in the chair.

"Yes, because ... Now that you're here it just seems more unreal." John ran a hand over his head. "A coworker told me the first part, because I live out here. I have a long commute," he told Chloe. "Worth it, though, to have my own place and not have to live in Lexington."

She nodded.

"Story was that there's a town up in the hills," John gestured vaguely to the east, "which is completely abandoned, and if you go there after dark there are … things. She said cryptids. I have doubts."

"Yes, wisely," Mr. Cruor nodded at him.

"And that would have been that, just a campfire story. Except that she could see I didn't believe her, and she told me I could talk to her granny if I wanted to hear the truth."

"So of course you couldn't disrespect her granny by not going," Chloe spoke up.

John turned to her, a wry smile on his face. "You understand. Last Saturday I went out and met Suellen McBride and now… I don't know, sir." He looked back at Mr. Cruor. "I really don't. Suellen told me a story of a family feud that spun out of control. She said the town had mostly been abandoned due to lack of work and resources, the same old story. Those who remained were scratching by, it's so far off the beaten path that even drugs aren't a big problem other than, I suspect, marijuana grows in the hills."

Mr. Cruor nodded. John went on.

"She didn't know what started it, she said." Mr. Cruor's eyes narrowed a little. "Yeah, I think she wasn't telling me the truth there. She told me they killed each other off, one at a time, then there was a last big fight and no survivors."

"You think she was there," Chloe said. Both men looked at her. "How else would she know?"

"True." John threw his hands in the air. "And she says the whole town is haunted. Which is your department, sir."

"Indeed." Mr. Cruor steepled his fingers, and the cat rolled over in her sleep. "Seems there may have been survivors; what about the children?"

"Well, that's where it gets really weird."

"Weirder than ghosts?" Chloe asked.

John made a face at her. "You take ghosts in your stride. I've heard you talk more to them than to live people, remember."

"I'm working on that." All the kittens were asleep on Chloe now, and she couldn't move. So, she settled for sticking out just the tip of her tongue at him.

John chuckled. "She says the bigfoot... bigfeet? Tribe, clan, family, whatever you call a group of giant hairy men... moved into the town."

"Ah. I see where your suspension of disbelief snapped." Mr. Cruor shook his head. "John, you know from your association with the Brotherhood that ghosts are a known thing, and indeed, not that uncommon. When it comes to elusive creatures, however?"

"Haven't you met Trunk?" Chloe asked from her position on the sofa.

"Yes," John admitted. "It just seems so wildly impossible that with everyone looking for Bigfoot, they haven't yet been found."

"Perhaps they have," Mr. Cruor said very quietly.

Both John and Chloe stared at him.

"Are you telling me ..." John started to speak, then stopped. "No. Not really," he protested after a moment.

"I don't know," Mr. Cruor told him. "I have not met one. However, I do not exclude it from the realm of the possible, as Chloe points out, I have a troll in my basement, a skeleton housekeeper, and gnomes currently cutting up a fallen tree in my garden. I cannot say there is no Bigfoot."

John folded himself down into a recliner and put his hands over his face for a second. "So I called you in to lay ghosts to rest ..."

"Why?" Chloe asked.

John dropped his hands and looked at her.

"Why lay them to rest?" Chloe gestured in the same direction he had earlier. "If no one lives there, and they don't want to go, they aren't doing anything?"

"You're forgetting the Bigfoot," Mr. Cruor murmured. "If they want to take over the town."

"True," Chloe admitted, pursing her lips. "The ghosts might make their lives miserable. Although I don't understand why a Bigfoot would want a building."

John shook his head. "We're all mad."

"Perhaps." Mr. Cruor scooped up the sleeping cat and very carefully placed her on the seat of the chair once he had stood. "I think it's time we paid this town a visit."

"It's not on any maps." John stood. "It was called Weeping Bride Creek."

"Oh." Chloe tried to pile kittens next to her, but they woke up and wanted to climb back up on her. "That's not ominous at all."

"Suellen said that was the first ghost, but nobody paid her no mind 'cause they knew she just mourned her husband what was murdered for gold in the creek."

"Gold?" Mr. Cruor raised his eyebrows. "In the Appalachians?"

"Yes, well, these stories don't have to make sense, do they?" John shrugged.

"I can ask her when we get there." Chloe had finally managed to get up. "But first, the necessary."

CHAPTER 11
AN EXPEDITION

Chloe came back out of the hall to find John putting a small bowl of cat food on the kitchen island. The mama cat hopped up to eat it.

"Escape while you can," he told her as he put a larger bowl on the floor. "This will only hold them for a couple of minutes! Bossman is already out there." The kittens had been circling his feet like sharks smelling blood in the water, and they fell on the gushy food with squeaks of delight.

Chloe, smiling, went outside again. It was chilly, but she looked up at the sky and saw that the clouds were thinning. It might even clear up. The leaves were still on some of the trees here. They hadn't come very far south, but enough, it seemed, to have stepped back in time a little with the season's progression.

"Sir?"

Mr. Cruor had opened the back of the Land Rover and was putting a long case into it.

"Yes?"

"Are there, is there a Bigfoot?"

"I don't know." He turned and looked at her, his face calm. "It is possible, if unlikely. If there is, however, I highly doubt we will meet one."

"What can we do ... with this town. Not Bigfoot."

"If there is a bigfoot, or feet, as the case may be, they are very practiced at eluding people. And as you said, why would they take over a town, however small and abandoned it is?" He stepped aside as John came out carrying another long case.

"We are going to see about the ghosts. And for Suellen, who seems to be haunted by memories if nothing else."

John closed the back. "Yes, and I got the feeling she told me for a reason."

"Because of the Brotherhood?" Chloe cocked her head. "I thought…"

Both men were shaking their heads. "No," John spoke. "Because of what I do for a living. She can't talk to the police; that's not socially acceptable here. But she could talk to me, who is adjacent to law enforcement and whose family has been here for generations."

"And the police would have dismissed her, anyway." Mr. Cruor pointed out. "Just as they initially did for the little old lady we recently met."

Chloe nodded. "You said that the poor little old ladies had other people they could turn to."

"Yes. Community, like John here. Pastors of churches, if there are any still viable."

"All over, but tiny and elderly," John put in, nodding. "Family is also dying out. As a concept, and literally."

"So. We are here for her." Mr. Cruor looked at John. "Do you know the way?"

"I haven't been there. But she gave me directions, and

clearer ones than 'turn where the old Johnson barn used to be."

"You drive, then," Chloe told him. "I'll ride in the back."

"I'm... ok with you driving." John smirked. "Boss says you have gotten much better at it."

"Maybe on the way back." She opened the passenger door on the driver's side and climbed in.

"Ok, John reached in and adjusted his seat before climbing in. "But you can't nap, so you know where we've been."

John knew the trick to starting the cantankerous engine and got it going on the first try, then easily maneuvered the Abomination into a turn before heading out of his driveway.

"I don't know exactly how long this drive will take," he told them as they turned onto the main road again, pointing east and away from the interstate, deeper into the hills. "Suellen wasn't terribly clear on that, since when she last visited, she wasn't driving, she said. However, I can say it's not more than three hours, or we'd be in West Virginia."

"And that time is because it will not be not good roads," Mr. Cruor explained. "I don't know that you have been in this area, Miss Brandt."

Chloe spoke up so they could hear her over the engine noise. "No, we vacationed in Hocking Hills, not so much down here. Other than one trip to Mammoth Caves."

"That's the other side of the state. Over here? There are some pretty state parks," John commented. "But no, you can't get anywhere fast. Although once you leave the beaten path, it gets real rural, real fast. You could be a mile from a town and feel like you're deep in the wilderness. The hills are so steep and the forest so thick."

"Is there kudzu?" Chloe was looking out the window

on her side of the vehicle at the passing fields. They seemed to be paralleling a river, or maybe a large creek, and the road wound back and forth through the farms with it.

"Not much this far north," John answered. "Down in Tennessee it's really bad. We'd never find a small town if there was kudzu swallowing it up."

They all fell silent for a while, while John focused on the drive. He'd brought a folding paper map along, which lay on the seat between him and Mr. Cruor, but as he'd said, it really only showed the main roads. Once they turned off that, he'd be relying on the old lady's directions of where to turn and how far to go.

"We'd better stop here." John was already slowing and signaling. There weren't other cars on the road, but you never knew, Chloe thought, and it's a good habit to be in, she remembered him telling her on the one lesson he'd given her in driving before handing her over to Eloise to finish the job.

"Last chance for gas," he said now. "Stretch your legs, bathroom that isn't a bush, sody pop."

John pulled beside the single gas pump. Once the engine was off, Chloe climbed out stiffly. She wasn't surprised that it took even longer for the two men to make their way out. Chloe looked at the building, which seemed to be a house, with a lean-to shed on at least three sides of it. One of them was the store, and she walked towards that. Inside, there were tightly spaced shelves with all kinds of things, from fishing tackle to car parts to tins of food like you'd see in a regular grocery. Overhead, half the lights were not working, so Chloe decided she wouldn't explore too far.

"He'p you?" A lady appeared out of a door from the direction of the main house. She was wearing an apron and wiping her hands on a kitchen towel.

"Is there a bathroom?" Chloe asked.

"Right through here." The lady, whose iron-grey hair was tied up under a floral bandana, led her into the house. "There you go."

"Thank you." Chloe felt a little uncomfortable using someone's private bathroom, but guessed that it was unusual for visitors to come by this place. The room smelled of air freshener, and when she washed her hands, it was using little soap shaped like a seashell.

Chloe hurried back into the store, and looked around again. There was no cooler in sight.

"Cold drinks there," the lady was behind a tiny counter, and she pointed to a bin to the side. "Got cokes."

The chest cooler was beaded with condensation, and the lid didn't want to slide open easily. Chloe jiggled it, got it wide enough to put her hand in and get a bottle, and then managed to close it again. Mr. Cruor came in, looked around, and went back out again. Chloe paid for her drink and joined the men at the Abomination.

"The bathroom's in her house," she told them.

John nodded. "This'll be the store for the holler, but not many travelers passing through."

"I will wait," Mr. Cruor said.

"And I guess I will too." John looked at what Chloe was holding. "Is that what the kids are drinking these days?"

Chloe looked at the Vernor's ginger ale bottle. "No, but it would have been rude not to buy something and this was all I could reach."

John grinned and shook his head before climbing the three steps to go into the store.

"How do you feel?" Mr. Cruor asked her.

"This place is private," Chloe told him, then shrugged. "Not haunted."

"Secretive," he agreed. "More of a 'move along, now' feeling than a 'get out and stay out' from here."

"Yes." Chloe looked around. She thought she could see the roofline of another house through the trees, and across the creek from the road, with no bridge over the creek which made her wonder how it had gotten there, was a single-wide mobile home. Around it were old vehicles and ramshackle outbuildings. Cows grazed in the lumpy fields by the creek. "No one mows, here."

He looked at the pastures. "Likely cannot without breaking equipment."

"Rocks," Chloe nodded, understanding. "We're closer to the bones of the earth here."

"That is an eloquent way to put it."

John came back out, holding a bottle. "Out of the nobility of my heart, I'll offer to trade." He held it out towards Chloe.

She looked at the vivid purple. "I'm not a big fan of grape flavor."

He looked at her hair and said nothing. Chloe started laughing.

"That's not the same!"

In good humor, they got back on the road.

"I have to start looking for the first turnoff in about a mile," John told them. "There should be a bridge."

There was a bridge, although Chloe looking down from her window could see that the road was barely wider than the Land Rover. She held her breath until they were off of it, then let it out in a whoosh.

"You, too, huh." John didn't turn his head, but she could see his eyes in the rearview mirror. "I don't think that was made with cars in mind."

"Wouldn't they have forded the creek with animals?" Chloe asked.

He grinned, his eyes crinkling at the corners. Then he was looking at the road again.

"We may yet have to ford a creek with this beast."

A couple of miles driving up the creek, but on the other side of it from the main road, such as it had been, and they turned again. This time they were pointed right into the hills that swooped up from the valley, so covered in trees that it was hard to make out the underlying terrain. The road was still paved, but the asphalt was crumbling and weeds had invaded the surface. John slowed still further, sitting up straight in his seat to better see the road surface.

As they drove into the forest, the road made a little jink. John slowed to a stop.

"Look there," he pointed, and both Mr. Cruor and Chloe followed his gesture. "What's left of a house. Old one."

"I don't see..." Chloe started to say. "The rocks?"

"Yes, there was a foundation, and see that bit? That was a chimney. There's soot on it."

"Yes?"

"On the outside means the house burned," Mr. Cruor said. "Since this road was paved, not all that long ago, either."

"Could have been a house fire." John started rolling again. "Could have been the landowners clearing up a nuisance since squatters and druggies sometimes get out this far."

They were off the paved road, now, and a few moments later, under the sheltering limbs of trees still covered in colorful fall leaves, they were driving up the creek itself.

"You were right about the fording," John teased Chloe. "Just wrong about the direction."

Chloe looked down at the flat rocks. "It's like driving up stairs."

"And about as smooth," John grunted. "Sorry, trying to keep it steady."

"Are you sure this is where ..." Chloe was highly doubtful.

"Yes," Mr. Cruor answered her incomplete question. "I don't think you can see them from where you are, but there are clear wagon ruts in places. This was likely the only place where anything other than a man on horseback could approach. It will widen out later. If it did not, no one would have built up here."

"A whole town?" Chloe looked at the steep hillside, barely visible through tangled brush that sometimes grew into the stream and scratched at the sides of Abomination. "And I can see why we had to drive the truck."

"Town is a relative term." John shook his head, but didn't elaborate. He was creeping them along up the creek, which ran down the layers of flat rocks in a shallow stream of rarely more than a few inches at a time.

"Uh." Chloe looked at the waterfall that had just come into view.

John turned the wheel and gave it some gas. There was a steep climb of a few feet, during which Chloe clutched the edges of her seat for dear life. Then they came out into a relatively flat place. A tiny rivulet of water meandered through it to the creek, forming the depression they had just driven up. Beyond that, there was the town.

CHAPTER 12
OLD GHOSTS

As towns went, Chloe thought, it wasn't much. But she could see now what had earned it that name. There were five houses she could see, lined up facing one another. Three on one side of a 'street' which was a short, flat stretch of ground now choked with dead weeds, and two on the hillside.

"This was formed by an ancient landslide." Mr. Cruor was looking up at the hillsides. "There must be very little sunlight here, even at the peak of summer."

They were standing at the bottom of a deep, narrow ravine. Behind them, there was a sharp drop off of several feet to the creek, broken only by the intermittent rivulet's flowing which had broken out its own echo of the valley, and allowed easier passage up here, to where the flow of mud and rocks had stopped. Millenia had passed, plants and then trees had grown and stabilized it. Some people had found it and decided it was a safe refuge. Difficult to reach. Difficult to leave. Both things had upsides to them for those early settlers.

"I was worried about a grow operation." John joined them, standing beside the Land Rover. "I don't think that's the case here."

"I'm not sure anyone could have found it without Suellen's directions." Chloe was looking around. "There's no cars here, do you see?"

Almost every other house they'd passed had at least one abandoned vehicle standing near it, against the hope that perhaps time and money could come into being long enough for it to be repaired. Or it had been stripped of all useful parts, and it wasn't worth hauling it off.

"Most vehicles wouldn't have made it up that creek," Mr. Cruor pointed out. "And likely what was left went with the last people to leave."

"No survivors?" Chloe quoted, her tone dubious.

"Not here, no." Mr. Cruor started to walk towards the houses, along the rutted track which passed for a road. "The question may be, were they buried, or left lying where they fell."

Chloe stayed with him, walking a pace behind him. John had pulled a rifle out of one of the long cases and was taking a long, curving path around toward the hill, and then potentially behind the houses.

"He'll walk the perimeter." Mr. Cruor explained to Chloe, although he couldn't have seen where she was looking. "In case there are tracks of use other than the way we came."

"Oh." Chloe turned her attention to the houses. All of them were rough board construction, with shake roofs. The ones on the creek side stood up a couple of feet on stilts.

"This must flood badly," Mr. Cruor gestured at the tiny waterway. "The hills are so steep the water just runs right off it, and flash floods would happen with little warning."

"It must have been a difficult place to live."

There was no glass in any of the windows, giving the houses a look like vacant staring faces. Only one of the houses was large enough to have a second story. All of them had stacked-stone chimneys visible; the biggest house had two. Mr. Cruor headed for that one, backed up to the hill, the furthest from where they had left the Land Rover.

"Would this have been the first house they built?" Chloe wondered, as they waded through the weeds. There were stickers in them, and she winced as one made it through her jeans. She stopped to pull it and its friends off.

"No." Mr. Cruor stopped as well. He was turning, looking at each house in turn. "The one next to it, the smallest. That's likely the first. See how crude it is? Some of the logs are barely shaped. The gaps would have been packed with mud. There's a bit still hanging in there, but most will have dried and fallen out without maintenance."

Chloe could see some broken glass clinging in the corners of windows, now. The oldest house had a door, and a very small window, facing the road. There was a porch, which looked like it had been added later. It was very warped and weathered, silvery-gray like all the houses. The only house which showed any signs of paint was the next house, the big one.

"This is likely the last house built. Perhaps." He looked from it to the house across the street. "I revise that to the house built at the peak of this place's civilization. The end may have been a lingering degeneration."

"Why do you say that?" Chloe asked.

The house standing across the road on its stilts was missing a front door. Mr. Cruor pointed, and Chloe squinted. Inside the house, she could make out a golden-brown refrigerator.

"I wonder how they made power. Hydroelectric?" Mr. Cruor stroked his chin. "A mill on the creek would certainly provide that."

"That's a color from the 1970s," Chloe said firmly.

"Which is about right." John walked up to them. He'd gone all the way around the houses and was coming down the street. "Suellen could be in her eighties, but I think she's just had a hard life."

"She might have been my age when she... left here." Chloe looked around again. "This place feels cold."

"Which ghost hunters would say is the presence of spirits, or some such." Mr. Cruor was picking burs off his pant legs. "In reality, there is little light and warmth in a terrain like this. It likely stays cooler than the lower farmlands all year long."

"And they brought a refrigerator here." Chloe shook her head.

"It's not *that* cold," John pointed out.

"Are we ... going to look inside?" Chloe was looking up at the big house. Here, she could see that one window was still intact, sheltered up under the overhang of the roof.

"Perhaps." Mr. Cruor started walking up the road again. There wasn't a lot of valley left for the road to go up, past the houses. "First, I would like to find their cemetery. It will give us more information."

John paced past him, nodding.

Chloe asked. "How do you know there's a cemetery?"

"Traditionally, a remote place like this kept their dead close. They had no way to transport bodies, for one thing. For another," he paused and looked down at her. "They wanted to keep their loved ones close, but not too close. Why do you think the road extends beyond the houses?"

"Oh." Chloe looked at it. The road had become less defined, although they were walking along a trail.

"Game trail," Mr. Cruor pointed at a small pile of round droppings. "Rabbit. But deer likely use this as well."

The valley had narrowed, closing in around them. Under their feet, the ground was rising, and becoming uneven. John had stopped less than a hundred feet ahead, and was now coming back, walking back and forth from one side to the other.

"Casting for the traces," Mr. Cruor commented to Chloe. "They may not have used headstones. Cairns, or wooden crosses, were often all they could manage in places like this."

She nodded. She couldn't imagine trying to transport a marble headstone like Belleview graves had, in great numbers, to this desolate place.

"Here." John had stopped, and raised a hand.

They walked towards him, though knee-high vegetation. Mr. Cruor stopped before they'd reached John.

"I see them." Chloe told him. There were neat rectangles of stone laid out, the stones from the creek, arranged over what would have been the loose earth of a grave. One of the stones at the end of the rectangle had a scratched inscription on it. Chloe dropped to her knees and brushed away leaves and some soil, which had built up over the stones, away.

"Prov. 3:21-22" She read out loud to the men.

"Keep sound wisdom and discretion, so shall they be life to their soul," Mr. Cruor recited back to her.

Chloe looked up at him from where she was sitting.

"I may be missing a few words, but that is the essence of the verses." he was watching as John approached, carefully not stepping on stones. "There are enough graves here to suppress the vegetative growth."

"Yeah. Is there a name, or just a verse?" John stopped next to Mr. Cruor.

Chloe brushed more detritus away. "Mary Lewis." She paused, staring at the stone. "It says b, I assume for born, 1726 and d for died 1774. Can that be right?"

"Yes." John sounded emphatic. "This area, the Cumberlands, was settled even before the War for Independence. Settled by people who had good reasons to find a natural fortress like this would have been, hole up, and hope the world outside forgot them."

Chloe got to her feet, dusting her hands off. "No wonder there are a lot of graves, then."

"I disagree. There are too few." Mr. Cruor had started to walk carefully around the flat gravestones. "Families in this area tended towards many children. Even if that failed, in later generations, due to lack of resources, a settlement begun as early as the 1760s, say, for certainly the good Mary was not born here herself, but would have been the matriarch or at least one of the earliest women in this area. There should be hundreds of graves."

"Some of the surviving children would have left this place, for work, to marry," John looked up and around at the high walls of the hills around them, "to see the sky."

"True. Still, something isn't right."

"Sir?" Chloe wasn't sure about her thoughts. "What if ..? We were talking on the way down about sky burials, and how bones take up less space than a whole body," She explained to John.

"Sky burials?" John looked up again.

"No, wrong tradition." Mr. Cruor had come back to the

two of them and spoke briskly. "However, you could well be correct, Miss Brandt. If they came up with a way to minimize space, they likely would have. Also, we are as far from the houses as we can be, had you noticed?"

They nodded. He went on. "Cemeteries were traditionally placed in liminal spaces. Not so far as to be difficult to visit and pay homage to the ancestors, but not so close as to afflict the living with the dead in transition to the afterlife."

Chloe nodded. He looked at her. "You know this very literally, but remember, most people do not. It is simply faith and belief, for them. Now, John, how common are caves in this area? I know that elsewhere in Kentucky they are very common."

"They are here as well; similar geology and historically, the Cumberland Gap was known as Cave Gap. So yes, I'd be surprised if there wasn't one or more close by." John turned in place, frowning, looking intently at the hillsides. "Of course, finding it ..."

"Do we have time?" Chloe was now the one looking up at the sky. The sun had never been overhead, but she felt like it was getting darker.

"We need to take the time." Mr. Cruor wove his way around gravestones, until he reached the line of brush that marked the uprising of the hillside. "Which may mean we spend the night here."

"There's plenty left in that picnic basket." John pointed out. "And neither of you have said anything about what we came here looking for."

"No." Chloe shook her head. "I haven't seen or heard anything like that."

"Which should tell you something, given how many graves there are," Mr. Cruor was walking along the hedge-like barrier at the forest's edge. "A trail here, John." He stopped.

John unslung his rifle so it wasn't sticking up over his shoulder and bent nearly double, carefully and slowly moving into the thicket along the path the animals had made.

CHAPTER 13
CAVE OF THE DEAD

"He can't go far," Mr. Cruor put out a hand, stopping Chloe from following John down the literal rabbit hole. "Wait. He'll call."

"I don't want us to get separated," Chloe protested. "What if.."

John's voice came from not far away, muted. "Cave. Come look."

"There." Mr. Cruor crouched and made his way into the game trail. Chloe followed once she was sure she wouldn't bump into him.

The initial thicket gave way to a more open spacing between mature trees, the heavy canopy overhead suppressing the wild growth to the edges where some sun fell, even in this place. Chloe found herself regretting not having packed a machete, or even Padraig's favored billhook, to hack out that opening part of the trail a little.

John was sitting on a pile of rocks, his rifle across his knees. "You'll want to see this, but it's not what you are looking for."

Chloe could already see what he meant about a cave.

There had been a small rockfall here, long ago. He was sitting on part of the rocks which had come away from the face of the hillside, which was nearly a cliff in its vertical rise. What remained was a shallow cavity, roofed by rock.

"See the black soot staining the roof?" Mr. Cruor was pointing. "This was used as a shelter for humans. They built fires here, and the smoke rising marked the stone."

The ground was smooth and packed, bare of any vegetation, and there was a ring of stones near the front edge of the cave, such as it was.

"Probably used by the peoples who were here before the settlers from Europe arrived. And they might have used it, as hunters passing through, then while they were building that first house," John hooked his thumb over his shoulder, indicating the valley floor not that far away from them, although they couldn't see it from here. "No bodies or bones, though."

"Too open," Mr. Cruor shook his head. "Chloe, come and look at this."

He had been wandering along the curved back wall, and now he was pointing at the base of it.

Chloe came up next to him, then dropped into a crouch. "A doll!"

"Likely this was a favored playground."

John came over to look. "That's not all that old."

"No," Chloe didn't pick up the little dolly, who had been left sitting on a stone, her legs sticking out straight in front of it. "Polyester hair, plastic head, the dress is made from scraps of an older fabric, though. Doll is likely from the 1970s, about the time Suellen says she left here. But the fabric ... Back to the fifties again."

"Again?" John was crouched next to her and looked puzzled.

"The last thing? Case? There was a quilt made of fifties-era fabric." Chloe stood up again. "I think I can guess why her owner never came back for her."

"Perhaps." Mr. Cruor looked down the slope. "If the children played here, we need to look at the other side of the valley. They would not have been so willing to play among the dead."

The three of them made their way back onto the game trail, leaving the faded sentinel behind them, waiting on someone who would never come again.

"We are losing the light," John commented once they were back in the relatively open area. "I think we need to make a decision."

"I don't know about spending the night here..." Chloe wrapped her arms around herself. "It's chilly. And a little spooky. Besides, the cats."

John snorted. "Can fend for themselves. They'll just be pouty there wasn't wet food on time."

"I could call Padraig," Chloe pulled her phone out and looked at it for a long minute. "Or not. That was dumb."

"No signal in a place like this." John shook his head. "Not dumb, just outside your comfort zone. You'll have to re-evaluate your assumptions. One of those is that we can't have a very comfortable night. We have shelter, we have camping gear with us."

"When did that happen?" Chloe blurted. They had begun walking as a group back towards the houses.

"At my place. I didn't know what we were walking into, so certain things went in the back. Including sleeping bags. You can even sleep in the Abomination if you are afraid to sleep in one of the houses." John winked at her.

It was getting very dark, so he may not have seen the face she made back at him.

"I would not suggest sleeping in one of the houses." Mr. Cruor was brisk and practical. "Rather, on the porch of the big house, with a nice fire. It will act like a reflector to have the wall behind us and we'll be warm enough to fall asleep after a bit of supper."

Since they had it all planned, Chloe gave up and went along with it. "There's cocoa in the thermos. Maybe even enough for all three of us to have a cup."

Since they weren't setting up a proper camp, it took very little time to get themselves arranged for the night. There was enough cocoa in the big thermos, and it was still warm if not hot. The old boards of the porch were hard, but up off the ground enough to make Chloe feel better about no mice scurrying over her in the night. John had a fire started in no time, and they sat on the edge of the porch with their boots on the dirt, soaking up the warmth.

Chloe looked into the warm flicker of the small flames and wondered where the ghosts were. They had been sent here, and what they had found so far didn't seem to be what she'd expected. Not Bigfoot. Chloe was pretty sure that was an actual myth. Probably born of men in the wilderness gone feral, and letting their hair and beards grow out. Also, the photo of a man in a gorilla suit. Not that she'd expected anything like that. Ghosts, though. The weeping bride, if nothing else.

Chloe looked over her shoulder at the closed door of the house. She still hadn't gone into any of the houses. The dead they were looking for might be…

Chloe stiffened, staring.

"What is it?" Mr. Cruor stood and turned. "Ah."

There, in the lowest bottom corner pane where the glass still remained, a small pale face looked out at them.

The ghost lacked resolution. Chloe could make out the shape of a face, with shadowed, smudged features, but nothing more.

"Hello," Chloe turned fully, her knee drawn up on the porch, "Can you talk to us?"

The small ghost winked out, like a snuffed candle. Chloe sighed. "I guess not."

"Likely scared it." John was still looking at the fire. "No, I didn't see or hear anything aside from you two, but it's not hard to figure out when you jump around and talk to nothing like that."

"At least there is a ghost."

John looked over at her with a crooked smile. "You sound relieved."

"It's why we are here?" Chloe started to unlace her boots. "We came here to help an old lady lay her ghosts to rest."

"Which may not be literal," John propped his sock feet on his boots, wiggling his toes in the firelight. "Ahhh."

Chloe followed his example. The warmth felt good. "You talked to her."

"Yes," John shrugged. "The feeling I got was that she is haunted. Perhaps more by her own memories of what happened here than in a literal sense."

"Trauma echoes," Mr. Cruor had sat down again. He passed sandwiches in baggies to each of them. "We, humans in general, can put it out of mind, into safe compartments, while we must live our lives. In time, it tends to find a way out."

"It oozes through the cracks." John wasn't eating, but looking off into the night.

"Then why are we here, if not to talk to ghosts?" Chloe asked after she'd finished her sandwich. There had been a quiet time, where they all ate and looked at the fire. She looked over her shoulder, but the small ghost was gone.

"To give Suellen witnesses." Mr. Cruor yawned. "And to tell the story of those she had to leave behind."

"She's ready to give up her dead," John unzipped his sleeping bag and rolled up into it. "That's why she called me to her, I figure. She knows what I do."

Chloe crawled into the sleeping bag she'd been given, fully dressed, and curled up with her arm under her head for a pillow. She wasn't sure just when she fell asleep, and if there had been more conversation, she was unconscious during it.

Chloe woke up to the smell of campfire smoke and coffee. Her nose was cold. She sniffled.

"Good morning," John's voice greeted her. "Sleep well?"

"First time I've slept through the night in … days." Chloe sat up, stiff. It was very chilly, but there was some light in the sky over the hills, and the little fire was burning again. John had banked it the night before, so it wouldn't spread while they slept.

Mr. Cruor sat on the edge of the porch with a steaming metal cup in his hands. His sleeping bag was draped over his shoulders like a cape. Chloe thought this looked like a good idea.

"Did you sleep well?" She yawned and sat cross-legged,

her sock feet warmly under her, at the edge of the silvered boards.

"No nocturnal visitors," John responded cheerfully, while he handed her a mug of coffee he'd just poured from the percolator sitting on a flat rock by the fire. "Not too hot, I don't think."

The black liquid steamed gently, so Chloe treated it with caution.

"It is quite good," Mr. Cruor said. "The little ghost has been in the window twice. Just watching."

"So you weren't asleep all night?"

"Neither of us were," Mr. Cruor said gently. "We each took a watch. I had first, then John has been up a few hours, since perhaps midnight."

"Oh." Chloe thought about this. "I should..."

"No, you needed to sleep. Even though you are young and resilient, you have limits, and you have not been sleeping well, as I know." Mr. Cruor drank coffee. His glasses fogged up from the rising steam.

Chloe didn't realize he'd been paying that close attention to her. She drank from her coffee, finding it was good coffee, and not very hot at all.

"Coffee would be hotter," John was saying. "But I made it a while ago for me."

"It's good," Chloe assured him.

"There's trail mix for breakfast, and some of Della's cookies." Mr. Cruor finished his cup of coffee. John got up and took the cup from him.

"I'll get that if you're ready for it," he offered. "All the food is in the Abomination. There are bears in these woods."

"Oh." Chloe hadn't thought about bears; she'd been

worried about legendary wild men and ghosts. "Yes please?"

"When there's a bit more light, we will see if we can find the cave." Mr. Cruor pointed across the rivulet at the far wall of the holler they were in. "Then we can head out of here, back towards civilization."

"What about Suellen?"

Mr. Cruor nodded. "Quite right. However, she doesn't know us. John will be the one to have that conversation, depending on what we find today."

"I feel like... Indiana Jones. Or maybe Evie."

"Evie?" Mr. Cruor tilted his head.

"She's an archaeologist, and a librarian, in a movie my Mom really loves. She has adventures in Egypt, and there are mummies." Chloe shrugged. "Not that I expect curses and mummies to rise up, here."

They looked around the pocket of green, with the warm tones of autumn leaves, and the weeds which were fading into blondes and browns, in the morning light.

"It's very wet." Chloe murmured. "I'm surprised the houses are still standing after fifty years. I wonder if you could fix them up and live in them again?"

"I think if you look more closely, you'll see that although the walls are standing, most of the roofs are falling in." Mr. Cruor shook his head. "Likely it would be easier to pull these down and build anew. However, there is little to attract a modern family here. No jobs. Not enough land to be self-supporting with livestock, and hunting laws to constrain the wild game this family must have relied on for their protein. They likely gardened this area as much as they could, for food. But still, they would have needed outside sources of supplies, and some way to pay for that."

"How?" Chloe looked around at the tiny town.

"Labor," John was joining them again; he handed out cookies and small baggies filled with a mixture of nuts and dried fruit. Chloe was pleased to see the bright colors of chocolate candies in the trail mix. "The menfolk would have left, to be farm labor or even further afield to work in mines or factories, then come back with supplies bought from their wages. Things like salt would have been vital, and impossible to get here. They may even have worked as hunters; the skill of the mountain boys at bringing down game was legendary."

"Later, cottage industry was a way for everyone in the family to contribute." Mr. Cruor nibbled at his cookie. "They may have made things like quilts, laces, all manner of artisanal work, which would then be taken to a larger market or fair for sales. The industrial revolution and mass manufacturing would have ended that, although perhaps not as quickly in this area."

"But mostly," John took up the thread of conversation. "We were poor people. There have been books written and entire government commissions dedicated to the poverty of the Appalachian peoples. A place like this, though? They wouldn't have taken handouts. Pride and stiff-necked. Which is why they were still living here two centuries later eking out a living in their mountain citadel."

"It must have been very hard." Chloe started to roll up her sleeping bag. It was still chilly, but once she started moving it wasn't so bad.

"Which is why I said yesterday the children wouldn't have stayed here. Some, sure. And in some enclaves like this, it got very clannish and weird. But this place..."

"Here, there was some pride of place, and education." Mr. Cruor strapped his bedroll tightly and set it on the edge of the porch. "I have to think the grave's inscription for

Mary Lewis meant this place was home to a family which had honor and did their best."

"Suellen was... proud of it," John said slowly, picking up both his and Mr. Cruor's bedrolls. Chloe carried her own and walked with him back to the Land Rover. Mr. Cruor was extinguishing their fire. "She told me that she really loved the place. But something terrible happened here, Chloe."

Chloe nodded. "I know. I'm not naive and innocent, you know."

He stopped and turned, looking down at her with serious eyes. "Yes, you are. Untouched in spite of what you've seen, perhaps because of that clarity of vision Cruor notes as your defining characteristic. I'd like to see that unchanged, but I fear..."

"I'll be ok." She put up her chin. "It's my job to take care of people, in this space between the living and the dead. Suellen, and the little baby ghost in the window, and whatever else we find out today."

"Yes." He stowed their gear neatly.

They walked back towards Mr. Cruor in companionable silence. There was a tiny trickle of blueish smoke rising from the fire, but it was sputtering out as they approached. He joined them, handing the rifle over to John, and they walked up the road towards the tip of the holler.

Chloe broke the silence. "I think the baby is in the house."

Both men looked at her, surprise on their faces.

"The little ghost, the one who doesn't talk," she elaborated. "What if, during the panic, the little one hid and died there?"

"That's possible." John looked disturbed.

"Yes, it is, because it would explain why the ghost is

tied to the house, and yet, it doesn't fully explain why no others are present. If they were taken away for interment, they would not necessarily be bound to body, but to place of death, in some cases. It is never predictable, of course. Simply note that a traumatic death can lead to a haunting where the body had been removed to a considerable distance." Mr. Cruor spread out his hands, palms up.

"What you are saying is that we don't know?" John gave him a wry grin and shook his head. "The one that gave me trouble and landed me with this odd job was not tied to its body, which was miles away in the morgue."

"Just so," Mr. Cruor nodded. "The majority of death severs the soul, which leaves this plane and goes on. Sometimes, however, things go wrong."

"Can it be done on purpose?" Chloe asked, puzzling over what she knew, and had seen, and what had been in the books she'd been studying.

Once again, she found herself the target of two surprised stares.

"Why would you want to?" John asked, having stopped to pay her full attention. They were close to the rocky path of the rivulet, mostly dry at this season, but not a place you wanted to walk without looking.

"Yes," Mr. Cruor answered. "It is not a topic for this place, to be spoken aloud where there may be restless spirits, but when we are safely home, I will give you a book on bog bodies and the theory of what they are."

Chloe got the hint, and kept her curiosity on hold for later. Aside from that, she also needed to look where she was going as they scrambled across a ravine writ small in the ancient colluvium of the landslide which had made this valley habitable. It was no deeper than her waist, but water had cut away the light soil and sand, leaving jagged rocks tumbled where they had fallen, revealed to the light once more. Or perhaps for the first time, if they had been deep in the mountain when the original slide ripped them away and threw them downhill.

They came up into the brush, but John had guided them almost into another game trail. Chloe, her hands on a rock to steady her as she climbed up into it, looked over her shoulder. She thought they might be right across the apex of the holler from the cave they'd found the evening before. Again, she found herself almost crawling for the first several yards, then able to stand straight. Mr. Cruor, behind her, had a little longer before he could stand and not risk losing his glasses to a whippy branch or briar.

"Oh, now this is promising." John was on one knee, brushing aside a layer of fallen leaves, still orange and yellow. "Look, there's a rut."

"Someone came here with heavy burdens, enough to need wheels for assistance." Mr. Cruor confirmed, nodding and translating to Chloe. "And many times, to wear a groove that deep after decades of disuse."

"They were burying that many of the family?" Chloe had to scramble as the hillside steepened and John moved faster in the excitement of nearing the objective.

"No," John called back. He'd found a flat place, and was standing on it. "They were digging coal and moving it."

Chloe and Mr. Cruor joined him at the flat table of mine tailings. John pointed. Draped with grapevines, a hole gaped in the side of the hill.

"Can't have been a big seam." John poked at the vines, then pulled some aside. "They must have been burning coal in the houses after they found this."

"Then when the seam ran out..." Mr. Cruor bent, and walked into the mine cautiously. He didn't get more than a few steps before he backed out. "It became the family catacomb."

He took the vines from John. "You'd better take a look."

John pulled out a flashlight and crouched, shuffling into the low hole. When he emerged again, Chloe went in. Neither man tried to stop her. Inside, she could see the cave extended upwards, and was oddly wide and flattened. Marks of digging tools showed on the walls and ceilings, and mostly she saw limestone, but here and there a dull gleam of anthracite reflected back at her. On the floor, though, were what they had come for. The skeletons were lying side by side, clothing still over the bones in places. Beyond them, she could just make out boxes, glittering in the light of her flashlight.

Chloe backed out into the light again. Mr. Cruor let the veil of the vines fall.

"Why are the coffins glittery?" Chloe asked.

John looked at Mr. Cruor. "She doesn't ask why there are dead people on the floor, no. Glitter."

"Over the years, minerals have soaked into the wood as it wicked up moisture. This has crystallized. That's why they look as though they are shining in the light." Mr. Cruor ignored John, and answered Chloe's question.

"I know why there are bodies which weren't properly buried," Chloe informed John. "That wasn't a surprise, it's what Suellen told you to expect, isn't it?"

"She told me there were no survivors, so who put them there?" John replied.

"She did?" Chloe put her hands on her hips. "She was a survivor. Maybe there was someone else who helped. Maybe she did it alone. There would have been a vehicle here of some kind, probably more than one. It's not here any more, but someone took it out of here."

"They were attacked," Mr. Cruor interjected. "I saw evidence of blunt force trauma and bullet holes in the skulls. A very cursory examination at best, but violence is obvious and I'm sure you'll find more when you do the proper excavation and investigation."

"No ghosts?" John asked.

Both Chloe and Mr. Cruor shook their heads.

John pulled off his hat and ran his hand through his hair. It stood on end. "I want a shower," he grumbled, looking off into the forest.

"Did Suellen tell you who killed the family?" Mr. Cruor asked.

"Yeah." John put his hat back on. "She said Bigfoot did it."

CHAPTER 14
MISSING GHOSTS

"Bigfoot used a gun?" Chloe followed John as he scrambled back down the slope.

"No." Mr. Cruor was behind her, as usual. "Suellen is either lying or has created a false memory. Either will stem from the same motivation, to protect herself."

"So, whoever did this is still around, if she's still afraid?" Chloe slipped and landed on her butt. Mr. Cruor nearly slid into her. "Sorry, sir."

"Are you all right?"

"Yes, just bruised my dignity." She got moving again.

"Yes," John had reached the bottom and turned, offering her a hand. "She must still be afraid of something. I just can't figure out why now. Why would she make sure someone found them and trigger law enforcement involvement? It's been fifty years and no one even knew they were dead, from what I can find out."

"Four adults, three children," Mr. Cruor started.

"Four," Chloe corrected. "Don't forget the little ghost in the house."

"Which may be connected to one of those bodies," Mr. Cruor pointed out.

"I just have a feeling." She scrambled out of the wash where the rivulet divided the living from the dead. "We haven't been in any of the houses."

"We haven't needed to, and now we need to get back to civilization and report this." John was twitchy, looking around the valley, his mouth a firm line.

"What will happen?"

"There will be a big ruckus." He was walking fast enough Chloe struggled to keep up. She fell back, and walked next to Mr. Cruor while John headed for the Land Rover.

"Sir?"

"Yes, this must be reported."

"That's not what I meant." She looked up at him in surprise. "I ... we ... can't take care of this ourselves. But the ghosts. That's the part I don't understand. There were supposed to be ghosts, and other than the little one we haven't seen anything... well, I was expecting *something*."

"As was I." Mr. Cruor shook his head. "John was lured here by telling him there was a crime scene. The embellishments were... just that. She couldn't have known we were going to join him, much less what we are. Still, given what we now know to be true, it seems very strange."

He didn't elaborate. Chloe noted he was walking faster, because she was stretching to keep up with him. Her legs were beginning to ache. She'd spent too much of the last few weeks warm and comfortable in the library and not working hard in the grounds at Belleview. She'd gotten soft.

John reached the Land Rover before they did, and at a distance they watched him walk around to the far side, drop down out of sight, then pop back up. He was saying something; Chloe couldn't make it out. She broke into a trot as Mr. Cruor stretched his stride with his long legs, far beyond her capability.

"Flat tire." John had walked out to meet them several yards from the Abomination.

"There's a jack and tire iron in the back." Chloe said. The spare tire was mounted on the front of the truck.

John had parked with the nose facing the creek, and the sharp slope they'd driven up. That was twenty yards away. Chloe, feeling superfluous while the men worked at getting the Abomination up and stable to remove the flat, wandered towards the creek. She wanted to see if the waterfall they'd seen ahead was visible from here.

Chloe didn't go down the slope to the creek, and when she paralleled it on the flat ground above, she came to another drop-off. There was a faint game trail which went over the edge, so she carefully followed it. She could hear the waterfall, but the trees and brush prevented her from seeing it. She returned to the vehicle.

They had the tire off, and lying to one side, and were getting the spare loose. Chloe had not been looking forward to having to do that on her own if she ever had a flat.

"Tire's been slashed." John's voice was terse, low. He looked unhappy.

Mr. Cruor's face was the flat calm of his usual state. Chloe had decided this was his mask so he didn't give anything away. He was standing to one side, watching the valley, the rifle in his arms.

"Someone cut the tire," Chloe repeated, trying to wrap her head around it. "But there's no one else here."

"There must be." Mr. Cruor spoke without turning.

"Yeah, pretty sure a ghost wasn't carrying a sharp knife." John rolled the tire around to where it needed to be.

"Don't wander off again," Mr. Cruor cautioned her in a low voice.

"I won't; why didn't you call me back?" Chloe looked at John as he grunted and lifted the big tire into place.

"I could see you. Had you started out of sight I'd have called you back," Mr. Cruor assured her. "We don't know what we're dealing with, but panic is never fruitful."

"Now what?" Chloe asked.

"Hand me those nuts," John indicated the lugnuts he'd placed near the tire.

She did, and he tightened them all down. Then he put the spare back on the mount.

"Chloe, I want you to get into the truck." Mr. Cruor spoke softly.

"What's wrong, sir?" She opened the door.

"Explain later." John, with measured slow movements, climbed into the driver's seat. Mr. Cruor had moved, sort of sideways, never looking away from the houses behind them, to his door. He opened it, and handed the rifle to John, who had cranked down his window. Mr. Cruor slid in, and John waited as he put down his window. He handed the rifle back, and put the key in the ignition. He waited, then turned it.

Nothing happened.

He turned the key back then tried it again. Resounding silence filled the cabin of the Abomination.

"It would make a grinding noise," Chloe said, very softly. "Something is wrong."

"Yes." John didn't yell at her for the wholly unnecessary explanation. "Something is."

Mr. Cruor got out first, moving to the rear of the Abomination where he could see the houses, and across the width of the holler. John got out and went to the hood to lift it.

Chloe debated whether she should offer to help, or stay put and be out of the way. She decided she'd ask.

John was staring at the engine.

"What's wrong?"

"Nothing." He looked at her. "Nothing is obviously wrong."

"Oh." Chloe looked at the engine. He'd walked her through how to check the oil and other fluids, but it was an enigma to her. "That's... something about this makes me think someone wanted to make it hard to find."

"Which seems bleeding obvious."

"No, I mean that it's buying time. Keeping us here longer."

"It's an ambush." He nodded. "I see what you mean, now. Which also may mean that they didn't permanently disable the Abomination, since that I'd have seen."

"What can be done that looks, well, normal?" Chloe was looking around. A squirrel leaped from one tree to another, but nothing else was moving.

"Plug wires." He bent over. "Thanks," he grunted as he reached into the engine.

Chloe walked back to where Mr. Cruor was patrolling.

"Nothing obvious done to the engine, so John's trying the plug wires." She reported.

"Interesting." Mr. Cruor's face was tight. "I have seen no motion."

"There has to be someone hiding, and they can't have driven in up the creek, we'd have heard them." Chloe paused. "I think?"

"Perhaps not while we were far from the creek, yesterday at the cave, or this morning at the mine." He shook his head. "Difficult to say. Still, if they drove in, where is their vehicle?"

"Closer to the waterfall?" Chloe shrugged. "I tried to see it and couldn't, although I could kind of hear it."

"There is also the possibility that someone was here. Waiting for John."

"He said something about an ambush."

"He has experience with them."

Chloe nodded, remembering that John was an Army veteran. "But why?"

"That's an unanswerable question."

Chloe looked back at the truck. John was still tinkering in the engine. The driver's door was standing open and as she watched he walked to it, stuck his arm in, and she guessed tried to start it, although she couldn't see what he was doing.

"Suellen sent him here," she said. "She knew he was going to be here, and alone."

"Yes. However, did she tell someone else what she had done? Her granddaughter knew."

"But her granddaughter works with John, so she's also law enforcement adjacent and would hardly have brought John into the... the drama, if she was trying to keep this a secret."

"Indeed. Not her, then, but perhaps other family. This was the Lewis clan. Her last name, John told us, is now McBride, implying the marriage, or even that she obscured her identity after she left this place."

"I wonder if she told John who the feud was with." Chloe realized that hadn't come up.

She headed back to the front of the vehicle. John was swearing under his breath, and he stopped as she walked up.

"I've heard it all before," Chloe informed him. "I used to ride the bus, you know."

John huffed a short laugh. "I'm sure you have, and I could probably continue your education, but I won't. What's up?"

"Mr. Cruor sees no movement. Did Suellen tell you who was feuding with her family?"

John blinked. "I was so distracted by the bigfoot story I didn't even ask. No. Also, the plug wires are not the problem."

"So, could that feud be... what's happening now?"

"After fifty years?" He looked skeptical. "I mean, we hillbillies chew on our grudges for a long, long time but that seems above and beyond even our stubbornness."

"There's so much we don't know." Chloe clenched her fists. She looked towards the houses. "I need to do something."

"No, you don't." John contradicted her, his tone harsh. "At times like this, you don't run around and work yourself into a lather. Don't do something. Stand there. It's the safest way, it prevents more trouble from piling on, and you don't wind up having to be rescued yourself. Second rule of first responders."

Chloe remembered him telling her the first rule, never to rush on a scene until you knew it was safe. She'd lived that, in the encounter with the wraith's nest, and if it hadn't been for Mr. Cruor holding her back ...

"I think I need to talk to the ghost again." Chloe informed John. "But I promise I won't go alone."

He straightened up. "I'm not making progress on the engine anyway. If you must, we all go. No splitting up the party."

Chloe led the way back to Mr. Cruor. "I need to talk to the little ghost."

He looked at John, who nodded.

"There's no one else who could tell us the truth." Chloe crossed her arms over her chest. "It sounds like Suellen may not even remember the truth, *if* she was willing to spill *all* the tea without adding in Bigfoot and hauntings. There is one ghost here. One. And I need to have a chat with it."

"Yes," Mr. Cruor surprised her by not even trying to argue. "John, lock up the Abomination, please."

"Wait." Chloe trotted to her side and reached in, grabbing her bag. "I have protein bars." She pulled them out, and rejoined the men, giving them each one. "I'm hungry."

"Thank you," John accepted it.

They walked back towards the big house. Chloe chewed her protein bar, finished her bottle of water and stuck the empty bottle in her bag. She was glad she'd put the flat of water in the truck. It was one of the safety gear things her Mom had insisted on. Always jumper cables, always water, always…

"I suppose you want to go in there." John eyed the house suspiciously.

"I do." Chloe walked up the step and onto the porch.

"I'll stand watch, John." Mr. Cruor was still cradling the rifle. He stepped up onto the porch, his back to the wall.

John pulled a pistol Chloe hadn't realized he had, and with his body away from the door, turned the handle and pushed on it. The door stuck.

"Dammit." He stood still for a moment. Nothing happened. Then he pushed the door all the way open with his shoulder, and shone his flashlight around the dark room he'd revealed, pistol muzzle tracking with the light. "Wait." He told Chloe, and vanished inside.

"Let him clear it, and he'll be happier," Mr. Cruor told her quietly. "He can't deal with a ghost, so this is his way of coping."

"I know." Chloe nodded. "I couldn't deal with a human who was stabbing tires, so I talk to the ghost. We're a team."

John came back to the door, pistol down by his side. "It's clear. You probably shouldn't go upstairs. Looks like the roof is partly caved in; I can see light through it."

"I may not have to," Chloe shrugged. "The ghost came to the front window last night."

"What are you going to do?" John asked curiously.

"Talk to it."

Chloe walked into the front room and looked around. There was some light coming from the two front windows that flanked the door. To the left of the door was a table, with two chairs standing at it. Others were strewn around the floor. To the right of the door was a couch, and two easy chairs. One of these had been spun around until it faced the back wall. Chloe could see that the coffee table, which had stood between the chairs and couch, was broken. She walked towards the dining table. There were dishes scattered all over. Some were broken, some weren't, so she carefully tried to avoid broken glass and ceramic. Dead leaves had blown in through the missing windows, making that difficult. At the end of the room was a China hutch, and behind the glass doors a full China set could still be seen, through the accumulated grime of decades. There was a doorway, and Chloe looked through it into the kitchen. An old-fashioned stove, the kind that would have burned wood -- or coal, she suspected -- stood between counters which were piled with debris. Something had gone through all the cupboards. A small refrigerator, the same harvest gold-brown as the one they'd glimpsed in the other house, stood in the corner. It was plugged into an obviously hand-wired and afterthought outlet that was tacked to the wall;

the wire ran out the wall to the outside. She didn't see anything else which would have used electricity.

From the kitchen, she passed through into a small bedroom. Something, likely mice or squirrels, had made a huge nest from the mattress and bedding. Chloe came back out and retraced her steps to the living room. The stairs were steep and narrow, and she looked up them thoughtfully. John would have gone up, and they took his weight, but the boards were badly cupped and moisture-damaged; some had pulled loose of their nails completely. She looked beneath the stairs. There was a cupboard door, and she put her hand on the carved wooden latch that held it closed. It seemed too easy.

It was. The cupboard was where the pantry had been, shelves below the stairs still holding nearly-black canning jars filled with unidentifiable foodstuffs. Brooms and a mop, with its bucket, stood on the tall side of the cupboard. Chloe closed it again.

She went back to the bottom of the stairs and lifted her foot to step on them, when there was a flicker of movement from the living room. Chloe turned, thinking someone had walked in front of the window; the movement had been more light and shadow than anything solid. As she looked toward the window, she realized that the couch stood away from it a couple of feet. There was a chest there, between the couch back and the window. There had been pillows on it, and possibly a blanket. It was not clear what the mess piled at the end of the chest had been before decades of rain and animals destroyed a home.

Chloe walked up to the chest and stood looking down at it, then she looked out of the window. This was the window where she'd seen the little ghost, through the dirty pane of glass which remained in the window.

"What is it?" John walked across the porch to her.

"Did one of you just walk past this window?" Chloe asked him through the gaping hole in the wall.

"No."

Mr. Cruor was standing with his back to them, holding the rifle, watching.

"I think I know where a little one would hide."

Chloe looked down at the chest, while John came closer to see what she was looking at. Chloe reached down and lifted the old wooden lid, the boards warped with the rain's harsh caresses over the years. Inside, there was a small skeleton, partly wrapped in a blanket, but with one arm showing enough floral print of a dress to make it clear this had been a girl. Her partly mummified skull was turned to the side, and long strands of hair swept over what was left of her face.

"Oh, you poor little thing." Chloe whispered.

The ghost sat up from her body, shimmering into enough clarity Chloe could make out features. She rubbed her eyes, and then looked up at Chloe.

"Have you come to take me to them?" she asked.

CHAPTER 15
BIGFOOT

"Take you to who?" Chloe was sure that was not grammatically correct, but whom sounded pretentious every time.

"Ma, Gran..." She sniffled. "I'm so scared!"

Chloe squatted down at the end of the chest, to be at the same level with the ghost. "You don't need to be afraid now." Chloe had no idea if the little girl was aware she was dead. Chloe knew there was no way any more pain or harm could come to the body of the child. Which didn't mean her own mind couldn't be tormented. "May I ask you some questions? And then, I can take you to them."

"You can't move a body, Chloe," John interrupted.

Chloe glared up at him. The little ghost ignored him. She had a finger in what would have been her mouth, and was clutching a dim object to her chest with the other hand. Chloe couldn't make out the misty outline, but suspected it might be a favorite toy. If her ghostly acquaintances appeared to be wearing clothes, she saw no reason they might not also cling to a lovey.

"What is your name, child?" Chloe asked. "My name is Chloe."

There was a long pause, then she heard, although the finger didn't move -- because ghosts didn't actually speak, Chloe reminded herself -- very clearly. "My name is Ginny Betty."

"Well, Ginny Betty, is that short for Elizabeth Virginia?"

There was a nod, and Chloe smiled. "I can see why they call you Ginny Betty, then. Is that your dolly?"

There was another nod, and a reflexive little movement as though she were clutching it tighter.

"Ginny," Chloe took a deep breath, smelling autumn leaves and something else, musty and sour, under them. "What do you remember?"

"Ma, Ma said I had to run."

"And you hid in here?" Chloe indicated the chest. "This would be a great hide and seek spot."

"She hurt me." Ginny whimpered. "She hurt Gran, and then me, and Ma..."

"Who hurt you, Ginny?"

"The girl Eben was courtin' did it."

Chloe rocked back on her heels. "Do you remember her name, Ginny?"

The little ghost was huddled up. "Suellen. She come up the crick and she said she was hunting and Gran said they's no game, and she said she's not hunting game." Another sniffle. Then she hurt Gran, an' ma, she said to run and it hurt. After a while's it stopped hurtin' but then I couldn't find them and they're not anywhere in the house but I can't leave it an ..."

The sniffles overflowed into sobs.

"Sh, shhh," Chloe did her best to offer comfort. She couldn't touch the ghost and knew better than even to try.

"It's going to be all right. I'll take you to them. You don't have to be all alone."

"Chloe." John was sitting or crouched on the other side of the wall looking through the glassless window. "What are you hearing?"

"She's very young, and afraid." Chloe spoke to him over the ghost's head. "She was injured, climbed in here to hide, and passed away here."

"You can't move the body."

"I might be able to get her to leave the house, incorporeal, if I can get her to trust me. I can take her to them."

Chloe wasn't about to break her promise to the little girl.

"I'll take her." The deep voice came from the corner of the house. John pivoted in place, a pistol appearing in his hands almost magically. Chloe couldn't see what had alarmed him. "She'll come with me."

"Don't move," John warned. Behind him, Mr. Cruor had the rifle trained on the intruder as well.

"Name's Eben Lewis," the voice said. "Reckon I have a right to do it."

"Eben?" Chloe stood. "You're Eben? You were courting Suellen?"

John shot a glance at her.

"The ghost told me," Chloe went on, pitching her voice a little louder to be heard by all of them outside. "Her name is Ginny Betty, and she said Suellen came hunting them."

There was an inarticulate groan from the man outside.

John stood, still aiming the pistol. "Cruor," he called.

Mr. Cruor shouldered the rifle and came closer, walking up behind John. "Yes."

"Can you talk to the ghost?"

Mr. Cruor looked down at the open chest. "I'm afraid not. Chloe?"

"She's still there, sir, but very upset and faded out right now. You all are scaring her."

"Been fifty years since another person was here." Eben's deep voice, raspy with age now that he was talking, or perhaps disuse. "Aside from me."

There was a brief silence.

"John," Mr. Cruor's voice was soft. "He appears to be unarmed. Let him come and talk to the girl."

"I don't want Chloe…" John's voice trailed off. "Fine. I'll keep watch."

"Thank you." Mr. Cruor gestured as John retreated, lowering the pistol to his side. "Mr. Lewis?"

The man who appeared in the window could have been Bigfoot, Chloe thought as she startled. He was very tall, and very hairy. Dark, deepset eyes glittered in the thick steel-gray hairs that composed beard and hair on his head, the whole mass of it wild and grown so long as to obscure his features. No wonder he'd spooked John. The rest of him was thin, with a worn plaid shirt and jeans hanging over his bones.

"I'm Chloe," she introduced herself.

"You talk to ghosts." He was staring at her. "You have purple hair."

"Er. Yes, on both counts." Chloe replied. "Ginny Betty is afraid to leave the house."

"I missed her." Eben was looking down into the chest, and Chloe could see tears appearing at the edges of his eyes, then soaking into the wild hair. "I looked and couldn't find her. Looked everywhere, I thought, but I didn't find her." He dropped to his knees, leaning on the windowsill. "Little Nilla, I'm so sorry."

"Unca Eben." The ghost was more defined now. "Unca Eben, I can't find Ma."

"I know where she is," he told her. "I laid her to rest with the family."

"What happened, Eben?" Mr. Cruor was squatting next to the big man, now. "What happened here to your family?"

"Suellen got in her head that... I don't rightly know what she thought. That I'd inherit this," Eben gestured at the holler. "Mebbe that if'n I had ties here I wouldn't leave it. She wanted money and to live in the city. Not here. She wanted me and she wanted money."

"So she came here and killed your family?" Chloe couldn't wrap her head around it. "But what about..."

"I wasn't here." Eben buried his face in his big, gnarled hands. The joints were big as walnuts, and his fingers twisted. "I was gone working. She knew it. She knew the wimmin would be all alone and unsuspectin' so she came here for them. I dunno if she was going to talk first, and somethin' set her off. I can't believe what she said to me. Can't believe a word of it."

"What did she say to you?" Chloe asked.

"I came home early. Came up the creek and saw her Daddy's truck parked there," Eben gestured towards the Land Rover. "Didn't know anything was wrong, not then. Came up the road and Gran... Gran was lyin' there." Eben's eyes dropped to the little ghost. "I knew there was nothing I could do then. I kep' walking. Found my sister on the porch. My own ma was next to her. Heard shouting and shots from the old house. My other sister Belle was there, with her kids, and Suellen..."

Eben dropped heavily to the porch floor, his legs giving out as he gasped. "She was bloodied. Had an axe in her hand and she was wild. She said to me, she said I was free now. Free to come away with her."

"What did you do?" Chloe asked when he'd been silent for a long time.

"I ran." Eben looked up, and she could see the wet trails in his beard. "I ran, and ran, and she tried to shoot me in the back." he held up a hand. "She did this with the axe, first."

His left hand, the one Chloe hadn't been able to see clearly before, was missing the pinkie finger, and a twisted scar extended well up his wrist.

"You had reason to run." Mr. Cruor's voice was just as soft and gentle as it had been. "You knew she'd killed, and now she was turning on you."

"Yes," Chloe nodded. "And then she shot at you."

"Missed," Eben said simply. "I got up in the hills, used my undershirt to stop bleedin' and didn't come down until the next day."

"And then you put the dead in their place." Mr. Cruor nodded. "To honor them, but you couldn't find…"

"Nilla." Eben looked down at the ghost, sucking her finger with big dark shadows where her eyes would have been. "Sweet as Nilla Wafers, used to bring her a box of 'em whenever I came home. Started callin' her Nilla. Wasn't until… a long time passed, then I'd start to seein' her in here. Called out to her, but she didn't answer."

"Eben, how long have you been here?"

"The whole time," Eben answered calmly. "I been here the whole time other'n sneaking out to get some things when I had to."

"Fifty years?" Chloe gasped. "Alone?"

"I had my family," he replied with simple dignity.

"Why didn't you go to the police?" Chloe asked.

"Couldn't."

"No, he couldn't," John agreed. The pistol was away, and he took a knee next to Eben. "Suellen's father was the sheriff."

"Yep." The old man nodded. "'N his boys were the deputies, then and later. One of 'em was sheriff hisself, later when the old man died."

There was a quiet moment. Chloe could hear birds singing distantly.

"Last thing she said. Screamed it at me. Run you coward, they'll pin it on you and you'll fry."

"The electric chair," John explained unnecessarily to Chloe.

"That's why she thought she could get away with this." Chloe looked at the little girl. "This terrible, monstrous thing."

"She did get away with it." John shrugged. "She had me wrapped around her finger, too."

"Why did she send you here, then?" Chloe looked at him, then at Eben. "What was she trying to do? Does she want the truth?"

All three men shook their heads.

"I can't possibly predict her thought process," Mr. Cruor spoke first. "However, I suspect she knew you survived," he nodded at Eben. "Because she included Bigfoot in her tale, and a glimpse of you, at a distance in this brush."

Eben just grunted with a jerky nod. "I don't let folks see me."

"Were you in 'Nam?" John spoke up suddenly.

"Yeah." Eben turned carefully to look at him. "Two tours. Marine recon. Lurp."

"Long range reconnaissance patrols," John translated

for Chloe again. Then he spoke to Eben. "Army, forward observer and radio."

"This explains why you were able to escape her and then evade notice all these years." Mr. Cruor stroked his chin. "Why not leave here and go somewhere with a new identity?"

"Couldn't leave my family." Eben shook his head. "Time to time I'd go away, work a little for some cash, but never more'n a month or two gone. Didn't want anyone here. Squatters. Ran 'em off."

"I see." Mr. Cruor tilted his head slightly. "Do you have a guess why Suellen sent John here? She couldn't have known John would bring Chloe and I along."

"You came to talk to the ghosts." Eben looked at Chloe. "You're a wise woman."

"Oh, I don't, really..."

"It's a title, Chloe, not an observation of your abilities," John informed her drily. "And in that, he's not wrong. You are a wise woman in terms of the hills, and it's better than being called witch."

"I'm not a witch," Chloe said firmly.

"Glad to hear it." Eben responded. "Suellen'd be... 'bout sixty-seven now."

"She was only seventeen when she massacred all these people?" Chloe blurted out. "Sorry, Ginny honey." She looked down at the ghost. "I hate that we're talking all this stuff right in front of a little girl."

"Nilla, you lay down'n go to sleep now, y'hear?" Eben looked down at the tiny body. "You take a nap, an' then Unca Eben will bring you to your Ma."

"K." The ghost faded out.

"Chloe, will you join us out here?" Mr. Cruor suggested.

Chloe found that her foot had gone to sleep when she

tried to move, so it took her a couple of minutes to join the men who had moved to the far end of the porch and were sitting on the edge of it companionably.

"I have a theory," John was saying. "I think she does still plan to blame Eben for his family's death. I'm not sure she even remembers the whole thing well enough to give anyone the truth any longer."

"How do you forget something like this?" Chloe asked, rubbing her ankle.

"Suellen was a good storyteller." Eben shook his head. "I don't know, I don't rightly know."

"She's a psychopathic type," Mr. Cruor said briskly. "In her mind, other humans are not individual souls with worth and value. Everyone in her life exists in relationship to herself and what they can do for her. Eben, this is not casting blame, but I would presume there was an inciting event which triggered her murderous rage."

"Wa'all…" The old mountain man drew out his words. "I've thought on it. Many times. What I might've said to make her think I wanted my family dead."

"You did not want them dead. She desired them dead, and out of the way."

"I don't know. I'd been to visit her family while I was comin' back from the war." Eben shrugged. "Her daddy asked me how big a house I was gonna build her, on a lot he was given' her next door to their house. I let him know there was a house ready for us, in the holler, I was fixin' it up. Brought in 'lectric 'n everything."

Eben shook his head and stared across at the other house, the one with the refrigerator in it. "I haven't been into these houses since that day."

"Where have you lived?" Chloe asked, looking around.

She thought she could understand the reason he hadn't wanted to stay here, not where his loved ones had died.

"Little cabin up on the hill." There was a brief flash of what might have been a smile, toothless. "Like a treehouse. Since there's no flat land I fixed it to trees."

"That would be fun to live in." Chloe knew his life had been anything but fun.

"You never married Suellen?" John asked now.

"No," Eben shook his head. "Her daddy wanted to wait until she was 18. She didn't want to wait."

"But you were receptive to waiting?" Mr. Cruor asked.

"She was so pretty." Eben sighed. "I guess there was something. I don't know if I remember rightly. I know what she is, now, am I takin' that back to before-times, to why I wasn't in a hurry to wed?"

"If you were off at war, you wouldn't have seen that much of her." Chloe pointed out. "And she was only seventeen."

"I didn't know her too long," Eben admitted. "Saw her when I was in town working a job. Knew who she was, wasn't going to say boo to her, until she started makin' up sweet to me. Walking on the street with me when I was goin' to the library. Sayin' I was a smart man, and could go places."

Instead, Chloe thought, he'd never left this dark little hollow in the hills. A haunted man, literally.

He was beginning to sound hoarse. John pulled a water bottle from his cargo pocket and held it out to Eben.

"Thank'ee." The old man fumbled with it.

"Here," Chloe recognized the problem. "Let me."

Gently, she took the bottle and twisted off the cap. "Your hands must hurt you."

"Yeah." He drank long and deep.

"Suellen knew you were alive, but that you were old and beginning to have trouble."

"Set on some squatters oh, 'bout a year ago, sent 'em packin' right smart enough." Eben shook his head. "Hands are worst in winter, but I can still handle a rifle."

"You shot them?" Chloe asked.

"Wa'alll..."

John chuckled. "You played Bigfoot, and flattened a tire or two, didn't you?"

"Mebbe." Eben's eyes twinkled a little.

"You sabotaged the Ab... the truck, didn't you?" Chloe was indignant. "What did you do to it?"

"Didn't want you to leave yet." Eben said, quietly. "Needed you to bear witness."

"You were listening." Mr. Cruor said.

"Ayuh. Didn't know who you were. You came right in like you knew the place. Knew then Suellen musta sent you."

"It was a chance to see justice done," Mr. Cruor nodded.

"Been keepin' track. Knew the sheriff isn't her clan. Didn't know what you are," Eben nodded towards John. "Knew you was with the police somehow."

"I'm a crime scene analyst," John told him. "It's my job to tell the story of the dead through the traces they and the criminals leave behind."

"Then you can tell my family's story." Eben sighed. "Don't know what moved Suellen to send you here. Providence, in His wisdom, sends you who can talk to the ghosts." Eben was looking at Chloe.

"Suellen was making trouble up again." Mr. Cruor folded his hands neatly in his lap and sat very upright. "She sent John into an ambush."

They all looked at him.

"She may have learned of the brush with the squatters. The wild stories about Bigfoot, after all, would have been juicy enough to make the rounds, and it sounds as though your coworker enjoys that kind of thing, John."

John nodded silently.

"She sends John, thinking she can use him to flush out Eben from the hills. Then, finally, with him convicted of his family's murders, she doesn't have to worry about that cloud hanging over her head."

"That's terrible." Chloe had a lump in her throat. "You could have killed John!"

"Now, now, I'm not that easy to kill." John patted her on the back, grinning.

"I don't hold with killin' folks," Eben chuckled. "You'd've been safe enough but mebbe uncomfortable if'n I did want you gone."

"She expected John to come alone, and to be easily manipulated." Mr. Cruor smiled. "She underestimated his capacity, as many have done to their detriment."

CHAPTER 16
UNRAVELLING

"If by capacity you mean willing to call in help, sure." John leaned back with a deep sigh. "Now what, sir?"

"We go away." Mr. Cruor looked at Eben. "And there are decisions which must be made."

"What decisions?" Chloe asked.

"Whether I report this," John responded glumly. "Sir…"

"No, you must report it, I understand," Mr. Cruor assured him. "However, after all these years, the scene is, as you say, contaminated."

"By every raccoon, possum, and squirrel in the hills, even if Eben didn't move the bodies." John shrugged. "Fifty years means no fingerprints, no DNA evidence, really, I don't know what there is left. Aside from the bodies with their obvious wounds. No way to say that Eben here didn't do it. No offence."

Eben shrugged. "I figgered that. I been up here hiding for fifty years because I knowed there wasn't going to be anybody could help."

"No one knows Eben is alive," Chloe pointed out. "What about..."

"Chloe, you can bring ghosts home with you, and cheetahs, and cats, but a human being isn't really..." John started.

"I was going to say, he could stay with John," Chloe finished as if he hadn't been talking, with great dignity. "He could be John's great uncle, or something. No one knows about him, not for certain, and would it make sense for Suellen to keep claiming Bigfoot did it?"

"It would not, but the mind of a killer is not sensible to the rest of us," Mr. Cruor reminded her. "If it were, murder would not have been their resort under pressure."

"Bible says 'thou shalt not murder,'" Eben put in, his deep voice solemn. "Means the heavenly Father knows the mind of man inclines towards it."

"Yes," Mr. Cruor agreed, "and you also know that the word murder does not mean simply killing."

"I do." Eben bowed his head. "It means the sin of takin' innocent lives."

"Which Suellen committed here multiple times."

The two old men stared at one another.

"There are other ways to justice than the law," Mr. Cruor said very quietly. "But to commit murder yourself is not the right way."

"I know it," Eben spoke slowly, his voice strained. "I wanted to do it. I never did. Don't reckon I will now."

"It's unlikely I can link her to the killings," John said. "Without you as a witness. But that doesn't mean it's impossible. There may be evidence somewhere here, with the bodies, with the... with Ginny."

"I'm willin' to testify," Eben said. "I ain't willing to die rotting in the dark."

"For a time, let John do his job," Mr. Cruor suggested. "If necessary then you could come forward. I'm afraid neither Miss Brandt nor I can be witnesses."

"No, the uncanny doesn't fly in court." John shook his head. "Eben, I think Chloe's suggestion that you come stay with me had better be the way of it. I want to know I can lay a hand on you when necessary. Also, I can update you on what's happening and..." John paused for a moment, looking out at the holler. "There will be a lot of disruption here for a long time."

"Yeah." Eben grunted. "Can I bury them when it's done?"

"Yes." John looked at him. "You have a family graveyard, we can use precedent to lay them to rest with their ancestors."

"You may never be able to resurface," Mr. Cruor pointed out.

"I been daid fifty years already," Eben answered this conundrum. "Let her think she got me in the back runnin'; I don't care."

"Do you need to set your affairs in order?" Mr. Cruor stood, stretching his legs. "Because we have had very little to eat and need to go home, we can't spend another night here without food or supplies."

"I reckon," Eben also stood.

"I'll go with you." John got up, and picked up the rifle, slinging it over his shoulder. "You'll have to move slow for me, old man."

Eben shook his head with a toothless grin. "Army."

"Marine."

The two of them moved off, walking in step on the road. Chloe hugged her knees. "What's going to happen, sir?"

"I think Eben will be able to avoid publicity." Mr. Cruor

gestured, and Chloe got up, walking with him toward the Abomination. "You will note that he didn't offer to repair the vehicle before leaving."

"Oh." Chloe hadn't thought about it. "We can't leave without him."

"Yes." Mr. Cruor walked past the truck, onto the slope down to the creek. "There was supposed to be another ghost, you'll remember?"

"Oh, yes, I'd forgotten." Chloe scrambled her way down to join him. He was standing on a rock in the creek, looking upstream towards the waterfall. "The weeping bride."

"A veil of water, falling forever." Mr. Cruor was unexpectedly poetic.

Chloe stared at the narrow fall, and saw the wind blow water droplets away. It did look like a veil moving. "So, there's not a ghost?"

"We have a little time. Be careful," he cautioned as he stepped to another rock. "Any wet rocks will be slippery."

"Yes." Chloe followed him up the creek. The water was very shallow, but when they got closer, they could see a deep pool carved by the relentless power of the water. It was very clear, clear enough Chloe could see fish moving in it. "I wonder how the fish got here?" She spoke out loud.

"Man brought them." Mr. Cruor stepped onto a tuft of grass, cautiously. There was a small shelving beach, where the water slowed at the edge of the pool, dropping whatever it carried, before curving around a very large boulder and flowing into the creek. Behind the boulder was a flatter area, where high waters doubtless flooded at times, but they could walk around it and onto the muddy beach. "Even before the settlers, the natives of this land would stock places like this with fish. They understood how to make sure there was plenty to eat when they came back, as they didn't live in one place, but had their rounds. They came back to campsites, like that cave in the holler. Settlers used those places when they came, but they didn't always move on. Some of them did, looking for the edge of a new frontier. Others, like the Lewis clan, stayed on."

"They settled," Chloe nodded, understanding. "And they fished?"

"They were good stewards of their land." Mr. Cruor was speaking loudly enough to be heard over the waterfall. "Or they would have despoiled the pool, and made their green valley a wasteland."

Chloe saw the ghost, then, walking out of the veil of the water falling into the pool, as the wind gusted and rainbows shimmered through the droplets, and the ghost's shape as she materialized well enough to reveal herself.

"Greetings, lady," Mr. Cruor did the inclination of the upper body that Chloe had seen him use before, in a bow of respect. "We come to pay our respects, and to beg an answer of you."

"You are a canny man," the ghost whispered.

She was a tall woman, drifting over the pool without leaving so much as a ripple in her wake.

"I have been called such," Mr. Cruor agreed.

The ghost turned her head, and looked straight through Chloe. "With a wise woman who is yet barely a woman."

"And barely wise," Chloe said. She meant it, too, she wasn't joking.

"Wisdom grows, child."

She stopped, only a few paces from them, still on the water. Chloe bit her tongue. Mr. Cruor had asked for only one answer, and Chloe bursting into questions would have been rude. Rude, and...Chloe looked at the ghost. Something about her had more gravity than any other ghost she'd met. The garb of the woman was clear, and old. Very old. Maybe not so old as the Mary Lewis who'd been the first woman to settle and to die here, but it was difficult to tell.

"We came to solve the unsettled dead," Mr. Cruor told her. "And found, unexpected, living still among them."

"You didn't even know there was dead." She shook her head.

"We were told there were," Mr. Cruor contradicted her. "By one of the living. Who you may know as the woman who killed your children."

There was a wild hiss that built into a shriek. "She left them dead and dying and washed their blood here! She knelt where you stand, with the innocent's blood on her, and washed my resting place red with the stink of the powder and the steel and the children…"

Her form had shattered like smoke, swirling around them both, cold and frightening. Chloe's heart was pounding in her chest.

The voice died to a whisper. "I could do nothing. Nothing. I raved, I screamed, and she stood unheeding and cast her weapon into the depths. I was helpless. I lost all hope. Until the boy crawled up the creek, burning with fever. I could quench him, see him heal, hold him close and safe. It was all that was left to me."

Chloe knew she meant Eben, who must have been in his early twenties at the most, then.

"The answer I sought you have given," Mr. Cruor bowed again. "And justice, with it, shall be done."

There was only silence, and roar of the falling water held no more words in it. Chloe shivered.

"Sir?"

He'd clasped his hands behind his back and had been staring into the water.

"That's the rifle." He pointed, now, into the deep clear water.

"It won't have fingerprints?" Chloe couldn't see what he meant. "Will it?"

"No." He turned away from the water. "John can see that it is retrieved. It is unlikely to be traceable through the serial number, guns were not required to be registered then. However, I think there will be something."

"How do you know?" Chloe fell in behind him again as they retraced their steps. "I mean, won't it have rusted?"

"Perhaps, but immersion in cold water is remarkably preservative." He stepped from the grass to a rock. "And I have a feeling. Such is what she called cunning."

Chloe subsided. If she was going to take ghosts for granted, why not premonitions? They worked their way toward the entrance to the town, such as it was. Or had been. Chloe lifted her head, poised on one foot, and sniffed deeply.

"I smell..."

"Fire?" Mr. Cruor, too, inhaled.

"Food!" She started moving faster.

They found that Eben and John had built a small fire, and Eben was skinning a squirrel off to one side. John was stirring something in a pot, and in a skillet there were something that looked like pancakes to Chloe.

"Reckoned I owed you a meal," Eben explained.

"And if he's going to be staying with me," John used his knife to flip over the cakes in the pan, "the food in his cabin needed used up. Mighty generous of him."

"That smells good!" Chloe informed them all, dancing a little in place.

John laughed. "I am remembering how young you are!"

She stuck her tongue out at him.

Eben slid the pieces of squirrel into the simmering stewpot. Then he headed for the creek to wash up. Mr. Cruor walked with him.

"Has he fixed the truck yet?" Chloe asked John, squatting next to him and inhaling the smell of something warm and nutty.

"No," John chuckled. "Your stomach is growling, girl. Got a bear in there?"

"I haven't eaten since this morning, and that was a protein bar." She looked up. "We're going to spend another night here, aren't we?"

"Likely. Won't hurt anything, now that we have food and water from the spring." John pointed his knife at a jerrycan. "Eben's supply."

"I met the other ghost," Chloe told him. "She was... different. Powerful. And she saw Suellen throw a rifle in the pool under the falls."

"Really?" John looked over his shoulder at the two men returning slowly, talking with one another.

"Mr. Cruor thinks it will be important." Chloe shrugged. "He had a feeling."

"I trust his gut." John put the lid on the cast iron pot. "There aren't enough plates to go around, but I cut some plane tree bark. Here." He put two of the cakes on a square of bark, on the smooth inner side, and handed it to Chloe. "No syrup, he said, nor butter."

"I don't mind." Chloe raised her voice. "Thank you for sharing with us, Eben."

"You're guests." The old man squatted by the fire and fed a little piece of wood to it, so carefully no sparks flew up. "Bread and salt. O'course, it's hickr'y nut bread 'cause I hain't got flour."

Chloe nibbled one of the brown cakes. "It's good."

It was coarse, and dense, but very tasty. She'd never eaten a hickory nut before, but it reminded her of toasted hazelnuts.

"I reckon I'll see if'n I can coax Nilla out just at dark." Eben was looking at Chloe. "She likes you."

"I'll come with you," Chloe promised. She paused. "It's my job."

"I dunno if this will work." He shrugged. "She didn't talk to me. She'd be there, looking out at me, but when I got close, she'd be gone."

Chloe couldn't imagine the frustration of decades like that. He couldn't bear to go in the houses, so he hadn't found her body to put it with the others.

"You tried," she offered in comfort. "And it really is my job, to help the dead find their way to where they need to be."

Not, she said to herself, like the ferryman. As a mediator, between the living and the dead. Just that the dead sometimes got caught and lost. Like Eben had been for so many years.

"Not used to folks." Eben was sitting away from them, turned so he could see into the twilight.

"Do you mind if we bed down on the porch again?" John asked, getting up and going to the truck.

"No, better'n on the dirt with the copperheads." Eben finished eating his cakes and stood, dusting off his hands.

Chloe followed him towards the house. She had left the chest open, but when she looked in through the window, she couldn't see Nilla. The little ghost had completely dematerialized. Eben stood next to her. "Reckon she's at rest?"

"No," Chloe shook her head. "She didn't wake for me until I opened the chest. Wait here." She wasn't going to ask him to go into the house with her.

Chloe walked around the couch, using her flashlight to keep from tripping on the clutter scattered over the floor. She looked out the window and saw that Mr. Cruor had joined them. Chloe crouched next to the end of the couch.

"Ginny? Ginny Betty, do you want to go for a walk?" Chloe called.

"Nilla, come out and let's go see your Ma." Eben took his cue, and called for his niece.

The little ghost sat up, yawning and rubbing her eyes. "Going to see Ma, and Gran?"

Chloe wasn't sure if she meant her grandmother, or great-grandmother, and both had died in the attack. "Yes," she promised. "Let's go see them together."

Wavering, the girl's ghost rose to her feet. Eben reached out his hands. Chloe opened her mouth to tell him that wouldn't work, then closed it again.

"C'mon, then, Nilla." Eben's gruff voice sounded from the darkness. The ghost, faintly luminous, giggled as she rose up over the windowsill like she was being lifted.

"Out through the window!" she crowed in delight. "Out in the night."

"Like an owl in flight," Eben told her. Mr. Cruor, with his red light, led the way. Chloe brought up the rear, watching the pale ghost walking, with one hand raised like she was holding the old man's hand. Just as she would have when she was six and he was only twenty-two.

Chloe kept her own light on the ground just in front of her. She didn't see John, just the strange little parade that wound across the narrow holler and into the ravine. Mr. Cruor moved with sure feet. Eben never stumbled, and of course, the ghostly child just flowed along. Chloe tripped, but managed not to fall.

At the cave, Mr. Cruor stood to one side, shining the red light on the ground where Eben would have walked, carrying his family to their long resting place.

"Thank'ee," the old man growled as he stepped into the darkness.

Nilla giggled.

Chloe didn't follow them in. She went and stood beside her boss. Somewhere in the forest, an owl hooted.

"They say," Mr. Cruor kept his voice very low, "That an owl flying by the cabin means death, if it lights on the roof, and flies off to the left. Straight on means bad luck until the first snowfall. To the right means all will be well."

They had left the cabin walking to the left with Nilla.

Eben came out of the cave, his head bowed. "I reckon she's gone. She was calling her Ma, and laughing, and then it just faded out with nary an echo."

"Yes," Mr. Cruor agreed with him.

Chloe didn't say anything about there not having been any ghosts in the cave. This place had other presences. The bride in the falls. She wasn't going anywhere. Chloe wished she'd been able to ask her more questions, even while she knew it wouldn't have been wise. A wise woman, the bride had called her.

They made it back to the campfire without any falls, which Chloe was grateful for. The stew smelled delicious, and the cakes had only stayed her stomach's complaints a little. John flowed out of the night and joined them as they neared the warm glow of the fire's light. Chloe saw Eben nod to him, and John nod back.

Chloe never knew what was in the stew, aside from the squirrel she'd seen them put into it. It was very thick, and she ate it carefully using the spoon Eben had cut from some more of the bark for her. While she knew there were spoons, and bowls, in the houses, she'd rather eat from the nice clean bark. They all shared the pot as their bowl. Eben's only bowl he'd filled with black walnut meats, which they shared as their dessert, washed down with the cold spring water from his supply. He poured some carefully into Chloe's cupped hands, after she'd rinsed them from it, and she drank it all, happy to have it.

John retrieved the percolator and coffee from their gear, and it added a good smell to the smoke of the fire, the stew, and the autumn leaves they were walking on.

"Haven't had coffee in a coon's age." Eben accepted the mug he was offered carefully, sniffing deeply. "Thank'ee."

"Tomorrow," Chloe said sleepily. "We go home. I do hope the Lert Cat is all right."

CHAPTER 17
REMEMBRANCE

In the morning, as soon as it was light enough for John, they loaded up the truck. Eben added a few belongings he was glad to be able to bring along. The iron skillet and pot, Chloe learned, had been his grandmother's before him. The morning felt lighter, happier. Decisions had been made, the little ghost was gone, and they were feeling that the mission was accomplished, although there would still be a lot of work done here. Just not by Chloe and Mr. Cruor, and Eben seemed willing enough to leave now that his last ghost was laid to rest.

"Ok," John propped open the hood. "What did you do to this thing?"

Eben, chuckling, reached in and popped the battery terminal connection apart. From it, he pulled out a long strip of clear plastic that had been wrapped around the terminal.

"Water bottle." He said, simply.

"Damn, that's a good one. Invisible unless you take it apart." John was admiring the connection as he put it back together. "I'll have to remember that one!"

Mr. Cruor rode in the back with Chloe, while Eben had to be shown how to buckle up. He'd ridden in a vehicle a few times in the last fifty years, but mostly, he explained, in the back of a pickup truck from field to field as a laborer.

Once they arrived at John's house, Chloe was woken from her nap.

"I'll drive home," Mr. Cruor offered.

They were sitting in the living room, kittens swarming both of them. For only four kittens, there seemed to be an entire herd of them.

"I can do it." Chloe yawned.

"You cannot," Mr. Cruor shook his head. "You need to sleep. I am old, and need less sleep."

"But..."

John walked into the room. "Settled Eben into the hayloft."

They had decided, while Chloe was sleeping, it seemed, that Eben would be living in the barn. It would be plausibly deniable for John, who didn't use it often, and Eben was still leery about entering into a house.

"Good. I would like to be back to Belleview as soon as we can." Mr. Cruor stood. "Call me."

"Yes. Often, probably."

John put out his hand, and Mr. Cruor took it, then pulled the younger man closer, giving him a hug. Chloe was startled. She'd never seen her boss do something like that.

"And you," John turned, holding out a hand. Chloe put hers up and he pulled her up off the couch, "You call me and talk about it, when you need. And you will need, you hear me?"

"Yes," Chloe was pretty sure she was going to dream about the holler for a long time.

"Take a kitten." John scooped one off the couch, "Here's

an orange. You need an orange. He'll shed the right colors on all that black you wear."

"But." Chloe didn't get anything else out. John had plopped the kitten in her hands.

"I have a carrier in the truck already for you. Sir," John nodded at Mr. Cruor and hustled Chloe out the front door.

Mr. Cruor, chuckling, followed them.

Chloe suggested she ride in the back with the kitten to keep him company. Mr. Cruor asked her to keep him company, instead, so she got in the front. Chloe thought she'd fall asleep again, but found she was wide awake.

"I have so many questions," she told her boss. "I know, I know, there's not always answers."

"Perhaps not, and some of the answers won't come for some time. Still, you can ask, and I can attempt to answer."

Chloe knew she couldn't ask for more than that. She took a deep breath, then let it out slowly.

"The bride. In the creek... was she..."

"More than a ghost, yes," Mr. Cruor nodded, keeping his eyes on the road.

"Oh." Chloe didn't know how to follow that up.

"She was a spirit of place," he went on. "When I asked about her children, I didn't mean 'of her body.' She may never have been embodied. In Europe, such *genus loci* were later called *aelfen*, which became elves. She has great power, in her place. But even she could not dent the armor of self-absorption Suellen has. If she had noticed the bride, the bride could have had her revenge."

Chloe blinked, processing this. "Is it about belief?"

"Not necessarily. It is about seeing through what is

assumed to be real, and then believing. Faith, in short, Miss Brandt. Suellen has none in anything but herself."

"I don't understand her. Any of the things she did. I want to ask her 'why' but I know that won't help."

"No. She may not even have a coherent answer, other than it seemed expedient at the time. In more pithy terms, of course."

"You said there were other paths to justice."

"Yes."

"Care to elaborate?" Chloe had turned in her seat so she could see his face in profile. She couldn't tell what he was thinking.

"There are ways to force belief. To tear aside the veil from someone's eyes. It is not pleasant, and it is not done lightly."

"And then, if she knew the bride existed…"

"Yes, she would know what she had done. A precursor of judgement beyond the veil that death obscures from the living. It would cause her to become unmoored, and I cannot say to go mad, as by many measures she is already there. However, she is comfortable in her madness. That would strip all joys and pleasures from the remainders of her days, brief as they may be in this world."

Chloe shuddered.

"What about Eben?" she asked, after a long silence of several minutes. "Will he be… okay?"

"Define 'okay,' Miss Brandt."

"Oh. Right. I mean, I guess normal life isn't really possible, is it?"

"No. However, you have an abnormal life. Are you unhappy?"

"No." Chloe thought about that for a while. "No, I'm not unhappy. I have friends, and …" She turned further to look at the sleeping kitten. "I have comforts. Eben knows his family will be remembered now."

"As he will be forgotten," Mr. Cruor nodded once, firmly. "As he desires. He will finally be able to rest, in time, as he rediscovers trust. He made leaps and bounds towards that just in a single day, by his own choice to reveal himself to us. He wants to be at ease. He will rediscover joy."

"Good." Chloe sighed and relaxed back into her seat as much as she could. "I'm glad of that."

"This is not an easy life we lead." Mr. Cruor glanced very briefly at her, and she caught the look of sadness on his face. "We must often confront the worst of humanity."

"I'm figuring that out. I never thought the monsters would be the humans."

"Some of the monsters are also monsters." His lips quirked a little. "If you can parse that."

"It makes sense," Chloe assured him, "and I hope I can live up to what is needed."

"You already are, Miss Brandt, you already have been. To quote a wise sage, speaking through the mouth of his character Linus, you 'hate humanity and love people.' In addition, you recognize people in any guise, not just when they look like you do."

The motion of the vehicle stopped, and Chloe woke up. She'd slumped into the corner of the seat and door, and had a crick in her neck.

"Home?" She asked, sitting up and blinking.

"Yes, and I see the tree has been cut down to size in our absence. I made a few calls earlier, when we reached service, and you were sleeping, to assure them we were perfectly safe and on our way home."

"Um." Chloe unbuckled and almost fell out as the door opened without warning.

Padraig stood there glaring up at her, his fists on his hips. "You were in trouble."

"I was?" Chloe wasn't awake fully.

"Yes, and also, you have a brownie."

"I do?" Chloe got out and looked at him. "I need to go check on the cat. And I have a kitten."

"Cat is fine."

"You broke into my apartment?" Now she was fully awake.

"Did not. Della went in." Padraig turned. "Come on, then."

Chloe followed him. "I'm not sure that's any better, but I'm glad she was able to check on the cat."

"She also introduced your Brownie."

"Wait, what are you talking about?" Chloe stopped at the edge of the lawn. "I thought you meant, like, can't decide if it's a cookie or cake, chocolate?"

"Not that kind of brownie. Although those are good. But only the corner pieces." Padraig waved her on impatiently. "No, you need a Brownie, and the clan asked around and found one that is okay with snakes and cats, and so you know, that wasn't easy."

"You'll need to explain more. I don't know what you are talking about."

"Little housekeeper. Shy, you'll never see her, but very handy to have around. Especially," He spun on his heel and poked a stubby forefinger at her, "if you go off for days missing and no one is sure where you are or if you're dead or something!"

"I'm sorry, Padraig." Chloe dropped to her knee so she was looking him in the eye. "I didn't mean to frighten you. I was perfectly safe. I had John and Mr. Cruor with me, and Bigfoot isn't real. He's a nice old man who's been hiding from the world. You understand that, right?"

"Well," Padraig turned away and kept marching across the lawn, which was rumpled slightly in places but otherwise didn't show any signs of having a tree fall on it, repeatedly. "Don't do it again."

Chloe followed him. The kitten would be fine in the truck for a few minutes, and she suspected Mr. Cruor was getting his own version of this scene with Della Dear. As Chloe and Padraig came up to the trunk, the gnome gestured.

"Looks pretty good. When we cut, it popped right over. Not all the way, but a comealong and some ropes plus a little excavation -- carefully, mind you, we were propping it while we dug -- and you'd barely know it was out of the ground. Going to be a heck of a fairy ring for a few years, though."

Which reminded Chloe of the bride. "I think I met an elf," she told him.

He looked up at her. "If you just think it, you didn't."

"It was my first elf? Mr. Cruor said she was a spirit of a place. She was scary, but also very sad."

He grunted. "Sounds like an elf."

The trunk of the fallen tree, upright once more, was covered by canvas drop cloths.

"What's going on with the cover?" Chloe asked him as they walked around. He was pointing out the edges where they'd reseeded spots in the sod, which had torn too badly, and telling her they'd used turf seed which would take more sun than the shade mix which had been under the big tree.

"Oh, that. You'll see when it's done." Padraig tapped the side of his nose. "Lochlainn had an idea."

"It looks like you've all done a wonderful job." Chloe raised her voice, guessing more of the clan was in the area unseen.

"Going to have plenty of firewood," Padraig said, gruff, and looking away.

Chloe knew him well enough. "Thank you, you did a fantastic thing, and in so little time. I expected this to take weeks."

"Eh," he rubbed the back of his neck and kicked at the grass with the toe of his boot. "Grass'd all die if'n we left it that long."

"True," Chloe left off teasing him. "I'm going to go get the kitten. And then I'm going to take a long hot shower because I haven't had one in days."

"Och, ay, can tell." Padraig grinned and winked.

Chloe walked off, laughing. She juggled the cat carrier and her keys at the top of the stairs a few moments later. She could tell as soon as she walked into her place that something was different. It smelled cleaner, for one thing, with a tang of lemon hanging over everything. For another, Lert the Cat was curled up in a cat-bed on her coffee table. He looked up and yawned, showing white fangs and a curl of pink tongue, then padded over to her. She set down the carrier, and the orange kitten squeaked. Lert levitated backwards a few feet, his tail bottling.

Chloe sighed. "So much for you two hitting it off. Ok, baby gets confined to the bathroom this time, and you guys can sniff each other under the door for a few days."

After settling the kitten, patting Lert and assuring him

that she was sorry she hadn't been a good hostess and wouldn't do it again, Chloe wandered into the kitchen area to turn on her kettle. She found a note lying on the microscopic counter.

In Della's beautiful handwriting, she read *'Leave milk on the stoop for your Brownie each evening. You are unlikely to ever see the Brownie, but if you speak to her, she is likely listening. She will respect your privacy. She reports to me.'*

Chloe looked around her tidy apartment and cleared her throat. "Um, hi? I'm Chloe. Thank you for taking care of Lert. The orange kitten doesn't have a name yet. The snake is Drama Llama. If you'd like chocolate milk, I'll get some chocolate syrup."

There was silence. Chloe had expected nothing more. Her kettle sang, and she poured a mug of tea, sighing. It was good to be home again.

The next morning, Chloe woke to hear the kitten mewing pitifully under the bathroom door. She staggered into the kitchen, pressed the kettle button, then went into the bathroom. She scooped up the little rascal before he escaped into the apartment to annoy Lert.

"Look, you," Chloe sat on the closed toilet seat and snuggled the soft baby to her face. "You need a name. I have no idea what your mother called you," The kitten blinked big golden eyes. Chloe sighed. "Probably something impolite, like John does."

The kitten kept his own counsel. He just purred, loudly, until she heard the kettle go off, and put him down. As she opened the door, she found Lert crouched beside it, staring.

"Are you going to be a gentleman?" Chloe asked him. "What am I asking, you're a cat."

A little later, as she was leaving, Lert was still on watch duty. He was fascinated with the kitten's paws, which kept poking under the door. Other than a cautious sniff, Chloe hadn't seen him do anything else.

Chloe let herself into the library, wondering what this day would bring. She was still tired and sore from sleeping on hard boards. Her own bed had felt wonderful, but she was not moving fast this morning, and wondered if Mr. Cruor was even going to appear.

He was, in fact, sitting at the table in the middle of the room, with a cup of tea at his hand. He looked up.

"Good morning," they greeted one another.

"How are you?" he asked, waving to her seat. "Forgive me for not rising."

"Tired and sore." She sat and poured her tea from the pot on the table. "And you?"

"The same. I'm afraid I forget my age, in the thick of things." He winced. "I suspect an air mattress will need to join the survival gear!"

"Sounds like a plan to me," Chloe agreed fervently.

"Speaking of plans," her boss changed the subject. "Padraig says there will be an unveiling after supper, at twilight? I am informed by both Della and Trunk."

"Oh, interesting, I suppose it's that late so they can come out and see it. The clan has done something with the oak's trunk." Chloe gestured. "They cut it at about eight feet? And right now it's wrapped in dropcloths."

"I hadn't looked. I saw Padraig ambush you, but after I went in for the day I did not come back out."

"Me neither," Chloe nodded. "I just wanted to be warm and cosy and under a *roof*."

He chuckled at her emphasis. "We were fortunate the rain held off. As for today, I am going to suggest that you take the day off. I suspect you have new roommates to socialize." Chloe nodded when he paused. "I am going to deal with any voicemails or emails, and then, I think, I shall choose a comfort read and a muscle relaxant. Ah, no, that must wait until after the unveiling."

"I'll check to see if I have emails," Chloe shook her head. "Which I hope not, because I haven't given out my email in a professional capacity. I wonder when we'll get news?"

"Not, I hope, today." Mr. Cruor was quite firm. "John is a sensible man. He knows that making a report of what he found on a camping trip can wait a day."

"Then the only other pressing thing I have to do is to name a cat."

Her boss's eyebrows arched up. "A complicated thing."

"Trunk named Lert. He is A Lert the Cat. Because he noticed the ghost."

Mr. Cruor chuckled. "A truly appropriate name. And for the small one?"

"I don't know. I was thinking maybe I'd look in the dictionary." Chloe got up and went over the big book, which stood open on its own stand.

"Perhaps another word beginning with a, to accompany alert." Mr. Cruor was leaning back in his chair, smiling, his fingers steepled together.

"Maybe?" Chloe flipped carefully to the front of the book. "Oh, after the pronunciation guides."

"Perhaps Taché, as in attaché?"

Trunk rapped on the door from the main house, then came in. He grinned at Chloe. "You had an adventure!"

"Yes, and I have a new kitten. Mr. Cruor suggested I name him like you named Lert."

"Oho," the big troll loomed over her shoulder to look at the dictionary. "Baft! Abaft, he is the smallest so always behind!"

"Dept, for adept." Mr. Cruor suggested, chuckling. "Perhaps not, as he is an orange cat."

"Dorable, as in adorable. You could call it Dora for short." Trunk suggested.

"He is a boy," Chloe shook her head and giggled. "Although that's silly enough it might fit."

Della came in with a tray in her hands.

"A..." Chloe was running her finger down the column of words. A bony finger tapped a word on the next page. "Anomaly? Nomaly the Cat! Hah! Thank you Della Dear."

The housekeeper couldn't show emotion, but there was a spring to her step as she serenely collected their tea dishes and sailed back to her own space in the house. Trunk chuckled. "He'll live up to that name, you know."

"Perhaps learn to walk through walls," Mr. Cruor suggested.

Chloe pulled a face at them. "I hope not. He's shut in my bathroom right now until the two of them get used to one another's scent."

"You should go on and spend time with them," Mr. Cruor suggested. "We can meet on the lawn at twilight. Trunk, Chloe is not assigned homework until the day after tomorrow."

"Are we still calling it homework?" Chloe picked up her bag. "I .. feel different about... everything."

"This is not a surprise." Mr. Cruor stood, slowly and carefully. "You *are* different, after the last few days. It will take some time to regain your feeling of fitting into your own skin, if I may phrase it that way."

"That's ... accurate." Chloe agreed,

It was raining when Chloe left her apartment just before dark that evening. She'd spent part of her afternoon napping on her couch, with Lert asleep on her chest. She'd played with Nomaly until the little fellow had fallen asleep, and it had worn her out as well.

Now, she opened her umbrella and walked across the shimmering rain-wet asphalt, which reflected the lights of the big house. Almost every window was lit up. Another woman in a gown with an umbrella came out, followed by a tall man also opening his umbrella, and finally the hulking rocky troll, who greeted Chloe with a hoarse rumble.

"Good weather for my moss." Trunk's version of a whisper was audible for many yards.

"I'm glad to hear it." Chloe was also glad she'd put on her tall boots. The grass was going to be very wet. She wondered how Della was going to deal with it.

At the edge of the lawn, Mr. Cruor offered her his arm. Chloe blinked, then took it, and felt him put a little weight onto her shoulder as they walked together. He was using a stick, with a knobbly top, that she hadn't seen before. He carried it, once he took Chloe's arm, in the same hand he was using for the umbrella, and didn't lean on it until they approached the oak's trunk. Padraig had found a pair of lights, and set them up to shine on the covered remains of the tree. Chloe recognized them as the solar lights she'd been using to illuminate the sign. They weren't very bright, but it was still helpful in the dark and rain.

"We wanted to honor Dolores," Padraig blurted without ceremony. "The clan owed her a debt. She welcomed us here, taught us to read and write. Old Underwood, he kept us on after … after she was gone. But it was her that gave us our first home in the New World."

Chloe blinked in surprise. She had no inkling of this. As Lochlain stepped out of the shadows to take one of the edges of the covering, she realized she should have known by how many of them had been eager to volunteer, as reclusive as the gnomes were. No wonder they all thought Padraig was nuts. He was practically a social butterfly, enjoying her company and being out in sight and all.

They pulled together, and the covering slid off, revealing a beautiful carving. A woman holding a baby had been hewn out of the trunk, not fully rendered, but clearly a loving tribute and recognizable.

"Dolores," Trunk murmured. "The baby was never given a name that was recorded."

"A very good remembrance." Mr. Cruor raised his voice to be heard. "She will not be forgotten, and now, her grave is known. She rests in peace."

Lochlainn ducked his head and retreated. Padraig looked up at the statue. He pulled his cap off in spite of the rain, and reached forward, touching the foot of the woman.

"She was like a mother to us," he said, then he too slipped away, around behind the big trunk.

"I'll stay here a bit," Trunk said, as the others turned. "Feed my moss, and well, think about writing this down."

"You should," Chloe assured him. "For the book."

"I'm working on it." He sat carefully in the grass, looking at the sculpture.

Mr. Cruor had been leaning on his stick, but now he walked with Chloe, Della in front of them. Her boss leaned over a little more and murmured, "I do believe she's wearing rubber boots under that skirt."

Chloe giggled.

CHAPTER 18
POSTSCRIPT

The bell over the door tinkled, and the young man behind the counter on his stool carefully didn't look around.

"Hi," Chloe greeted him. "How did the exam go?"

He jolted a little, and sat up straight. "Oh, it's you!"

"Were you expecting someone else?" She looked around the small, obviously empty store.

"Well, no, just... sometimes, there's a customer that comes in about this time. From up the hill." He'd lowered his voice for that part.

One of the old fluorescent tubes over the cooler flickered. They both looked at it. It went out. The other tube had been out for as long as the young man had worked there.

"Your boss doesn't do maintenance, does he?" Chloe commented as she pulled open the cooler door and grabbed a Liquid Death energy drink. "At least it's cold..."

The bell over the door tinkled. The cashier froze, his back to the door. Chloe could see that his eyes were very wide. She looked from him to the customer that had just walked in. Well. Shuffled in. There were a few wet, dead leaves on the floor in its wake.

"Ah," Chloe said, relaxing.

The customer, hunched and dragging one foot slightly, nodded, and moved past her for the cooler. Chloe picked up a packet of chips and came up to the counter.

The cashier hissed while ringing her up. "You know... that? What is it?"

"Do you actually want to know?" Chloe pushed a bill across the counter. The other customer came up behind her, politely waiting, a bottle of grape soda in its hand.

"Um."

"Didn't think so," Chloe replied cheerfully. "Put that drink on my bill too, won't you?" As he did, she asked again. "So, did you pass the exam?"

The customer ducked its head in a nod and moved away, out the door, the cashier staring at it the whole way. As the door closed behind it, they could both hear the breathy voice wishing them to have a dead night.

"Y-yeah?"

"Good for you." Chloe collected her items, and leaned over the counter to whisper conspiratorially. "Don't worry, a dead night is just a boring one. Trust me, that can be a good thing."

She walked out the door, making the bells bounce and jingle, and caught up to the other customer as it made its way slowly up the hill towards Belleview.

About the Author

Cedar Sanderson is an author, artist, and scientist. She has fourteen novels in print, and numberless shorter works, she can't keep track of them all. She lives in northern Texas with her husband and a cat named Lightly Toasted Marshmallow. You can find her art, fiction snips, and recipes at www.cedarwrites.com.

Also by Cedar Sanderson

ALSO IN THIS SERIES:

The Groundskeeper: Raking up the Dead

The Groundskeeper: The Hoodoo that You Do

The Groundskeeper: My Ghoul

The Groundskeeper: Deadhead

SLIGHTLY CONNECTED:

Lab Gremlins

Possum Creek Massacre

OTHER SERIES BY CEDAR SANDERSON:

Pixie Noir

Three books set both in our world and Underhill

Vulcan's Kittens

A young adult duology enjoyed by readers of all ages

Tanager's Fledglings

The first two books in a space opera trilogy, book three will be released soon!

AND NOW FOR SOMETHING REALLY DIFFERENT:

Running Into Time

The Case of the Perambulating Hatrack

YOU MIGHT ALSO LIKE...

DUST OF THE OCEAN

By Dorothy Grant

In the ruins of an ancient alien city, a half-alien slave's act of mercy will change the course of a cold war.

When Mika saves Arkady, a wounded enemy soldier, he offers her a path to freedom. All it will take is finding a hidden artifact that may alter the course of an interstellar conflict...

But the path there will plunge their team into the depths of inhuman nightmares, battling ancient bioweapons and outwitting her former owners. It's going to take everything they have just to survive, much less escape with their prize!

FAMILIAR TALES

By Alma Boykin

Welcome to a world where Familiars choose magic

workers, and a few others, as their partners. A world of adventure, tax-deductions, bad publisher tricks, and odd veterinary clinics, where wolverines wear glasses and iguanas sing along with the radio—badly—while casting spells and keeping their chosen humans out of mischief.

Or try to.

RIMWORLD: INTO THE GREEN

By J.L. Curtis

After a chance encounter with Dragoons and Traders turns a routine planet exploration into a rout that kills his team and his career, Lieutenant Ethan Fargo, medically retired, wants nothing more than to hole up in the backwater Rimworld he'd explored and enjoy a quiet retirement far from people or problems.

Unfortunately, he's about to find out that he's not as retired as he wants to be, and that his new home system comes with dangers, politics, and Dragoon sightings of its own. What promised to be a boring retirement will turn out to be anything but.

STAND ALONE (WOLFHOUNDS BOOK 1)

By John Van Stry

Chase had it all planned out, do a little time in one of the emperor's jails, say a four year stretch for getting rid of some trash that no one would miss, and when he got out, the path to the leadership would be wide open. It wasn't enough to be one of the gang's rising stars, or better lieutenants, he needed jail time, serious jail time — not that juvie crap or just going to county, to garner the respect he needed and deserved.

Unfortunately his bastard of a father, the same one that left his mother to die in poverty and him to run wild on the streets took an interest. Seeing him sitting on the bench when his case went to court was a shock. But not as big a shock as being sentenced to ten years in the Imperial Navy.

CECIL THE COMBAT WOMBAT

By Kelly Grayson

He didn't ask for cartilaginous ass plates, but military science made him a warrior. And late at night when the nightmares come of innocents killed or twerking an enemy to death in a dark tunnel, he tells himself he did it to protect the other wombats in his unit. He sucks it up, soldiers on and does his duty.

He's Cecil the Combat Wombat, and he's seen some shit, man.

Made in the USA
Coppell, TX
21 January 2026